PIXIE DUST

POETRY FOR
THE YOUNG AT HEART

Mary Martina Dockter

ISBN 9781959895107 (paperback)
ISBN 9781959895114 (hardcover)
ISBN 9781959895091 (eBook)

Printed in the United States of America

DEDICATED TO MY
CHILDREN AND
GRANDCHILDREN
I LOVE YOU DEARLY

TABLE OF CONTENTS

CHAPTER ONE

CHERISH CHILDHOOD

PIXIE DUST

Fairies live here on earth.

It is known small at birth.

With their wings they fly.

Flutter high out from eye.

No one sees, but believes.

In their magic conceived.

So to all by we must trust.

Be their spell of pixie dust.

2021

YOUNG AT HEART

Days go by faster than one can count.

Before you know it, time's in amount.

Larger than one wish the number be.

Wasn't it yesterday, you were just tiny.

And playing games and joking around.

Being free, living life a way it's bound.

Its freedom of youth not meant to part.

If one lives their life, be young at heart.

2021

CHERISH CHILDHOOD

Cherish childhood,
As youth stood,
And life will send,
Dreams to begin!

2021

TALES FROM THE CRIB

This is a story from a baby's dream, a story of
fairies and their magical schemes.
As this tiny tyke is laid in his bed, he quickly
closes his eyes, for above his head.
Are fluttering wings that swing in his sight,
for it's a scary sight when it is night.
And he covers with covers to cover his eyes,
so he doesn't see them, come alive.
He tries to cry but nothing is said, for soon
he realizes that he's asleep in his bed.
For mommy and daddy are nowhere in sight,
he's alone in a dream with its fright.
So he takes a rattle for a sword and he rattles
and rattles his loud weapon towards.
This small creature flying above his head, but
instead of dread he's now being lead.
To a magical place where fairies are found,
these magical fairies are flying around.
And take his hand so he can fly too, why he's
flying around with these fairies who.
Have, sprinkled a dust with their trust, a magic
dust from Tinker Bell's pixie dust.
As this tiny tyke is back in his bed, he quickly
opens his eyes, for above his head.
Are fluttering wings that swing in his sight,
for it's a lovely sight when it is night.
He uncovers his covers to see with his eyes,
for he wants to see them, come alive.
For this is a story from a baby's dream, a story
of fairies and their magic schemes.

2021

THE CHANGE

I rose one day and I was not the same
I do not remember when
The change came about

Did I slumber through the days
Believing fate would bend
The rules of life in years' amount

I was but a child was I naught
Yesterdays when I slept
But the days were added on

This will not happen to me I thought
A child I want to be I wept
My years of youth alas gone

Grown I am now
No longer a child in youth
I awoke to this new strife

With the change no warning allowed
A silence is kept to the truth
When entering into adult life

2002

MARY MARTINA DOCKTER

START CLAPPING

Silly me to think fairies are not real
With this belief has fate been sealed

I am guilty with many more before
What is not seen, must be only lore

But it is not a dream they are seen
With a fluttering, angel like, wings

As they whisper in one's ear a plea
If one is hurt, or is sick by a disease

For this fairy can come back to life
When, you believe in magical might

And start clapping with all your joy
By knowing fairies are real to enjoy

2021

PETER PAN PHILOSOPHY

I do believe James Barrie
In open windows

I do believe in Peter
In ageless shadows

I do believe in Wendy
In a mother sings

I do believe in fairies
In dust and wings

I do believe in lost boys
In the good within

I do believe in pirates
In one's evil sin

I do believe in Indians
In the wind knows

I do believe James Barrie
In open windows

2005

MARY MARTINA DOCKTER

A MOTHER'S PRAYER

From the time a child is born.
And long to when they're grown.
A mother will keep you warm.
Within her heart you'll be known.
For God will hear her prayers.
The many blessings she will say.
I will place them in your care.
Please look after them today.
By, granting me the guidance.
As I protect them in your place.
I pray I'm blest with patience.
And love for them upon my face.

2020

LITTLE ONES

We may be unable to see you, or hear you, or touch you.
But, you are able to see light, hear sound, and feel touch.

We may be unable to communicate that we all love you.
But, you are able to communicate, just kicking so much.

We may be unable to wait these nine months just for you.
But, you are able to wait you are so warm until you come.

We may be unable to know a time when birth is for you.
But, you will let us know when it is time, our little ones.

2009

MARY MARTINA DOCKTER

SWEET PEA

(Baby to be)

You're just a sweet pea, inside pod's tomb
The day conceived within mother's womb
As your fingers and toes, begin to grow
Your mommy and daddy do wish to know
A beautiful girl is their soon baby to be
For, they'll name you dearly our sweet pea

2011

YOU'RE MY MOTHER

A baby kangaroo pops its head out,
And looks about with wonder and shouts,
"You're my mother," best mom ever,
For I've been warm in this pouch forever.

A baby monkey jumps tree from tree,
But makes sure that its mom is able to see,
"You're my mother," best mom of all,
For you are there making sure I won't fall.

A baby calf walks away from the herd,
When glances back then moos to be heard,
"You're my mother," best mom for milk,
For since my first day it's as smooth as silk.

A baby kitten purrs as it is being licked,
As it is just born and cleaned not to be sick,
"You're my mother," mom with a tongue,
For, you'll give me a bath when I am young.

A baby puppy barks and when it tries,
It wants to make sure it is heard and it cries,
"You're my mother, and sniffs her out,
For, I can smell many smells with my snout.

A baby bear cub climbs on a tree limb,
Because it is there life's lessons will begin,
"You're my mother," a buzzing in its ear,
For it is learning a trick to get honey so near.

MARY MARTINA DOCKTER

A baby lion cub lies still in the tall grass,
It is watching and learning when it is asked,
"You're my mother," like an eagle will soar,
For it is not making a sound, not even a roar.

A baby raccoon on the beach by a river,
It is washing its hands so clean, every sliver,
"You're my mother," good hygiene taught,
For our food is found in the woods not bought.

A baby bird peeks over its bird's nest,
Trying to find courage to leave like the rest,
"You're my mother," to show just how,
For, I am able to fly, with confidence, now.

A baby duckling swims into the deep,
It is there it, splashes and splashes to keep,
You're my mother," swimming so fast,
For you'll look back and slow down at last.

A baby colt is trying to gallop along,
Trying to keep up with other horses strong,
"You're my mother," the best of mares,
For when it comes to mares none compares.

2021

JUST LIKE YOU

Mommy carried you within
As a kangaroo's Joey is in
Just like you, nurtured until born

An infant in my arms
As a baby monkey holding on
Just like you, wanting to be warm

Nursing with love
As a calf nuzzles above
Just like you, with your mother

Your eyes no longer blind
As a kitten seeing for the first time
Just like you, a world full of wonder

Turning over where you lay
As a puppy rolling over at play
Just like you, discovering the new

Sitting without a tumble
As a bear cub learns not to fumble
Just like you, able to see around you

Crawling to explore
As a lion cub searches for adventure
Just like you, seeking all out

Eating with your hands
As a young raccoon understands
Just like you, what they're about

Mamma was your first word
As a song from a young bird
Just like you, chatter can begin

Splashing in the water
As a duck shows her son and daughter
Just like you, how to swim

Your struggle to walk begun
As a newborn colt has done
Just like you, soon will run

And with other children they
As all baby animals, play
Just like you, together have fun

1980

PLUMS AND ROSES

For Mother's Day will always have a special place in my heart.

As I remember memories of my mother so dear from the start.

My sister and I would gather wild flowers growing in the field.

And picking only the reddest clusters Mother Nature did yield.

With our tiny fingers caressing the gift anxious to take it home.

But it was never complete until we picked the ripe fruit grown.

For two little girls hurried home, with smiles and runny noses.

Who, proudly gave a Mother's Day gift of plums and red roses.

2012

TO BE A HERO

A little boy sat with his daddy on his knee.
And, together they sat watching their T.V.
Some time had passed by without a sound.
When, suddenly his son had turned around.
"Why do you like watching sports so much?
Are they like a hero to look up to as such?"
His father couldn't believe words in his ear.
It troubled him so and brought him to tears.
He held his son tight, quietly telling him no.
"They're not to look up to watching them go.
They may be fast, hard workers for the team.
But their appearance son is not what it seems.
To be a hero one does not know that they are.
Those on T.V. think they already are a star."
He pointed to the kitchen as his wife was near.
Washing supper dishes as a table was cleared.
"Do you see your mom working hard for us all?
She is our silent hero for she has taken the call.
For, a mother is there when all others are not.
She cares about a son while players are bought."
A little boy climbed down off his daddy's knee.
He ran into the kitchen so his mother could see.
And he wrapped his arms tight around her waist.
With tears in his eyes words came without haste.
"I love you mommy," as he drew her in near, so.
To then whisper in her ear, "You are my hero."

2009

A FATHER'S LOVE

It's stronger than the strongest bond
That holds together, never broken gone

Deeper than the deepest, blue sea
That swims aquatic life, living free

Higher than the highest mount
That touches the wondrous sky no doubt

Brighter than the brightest, twinkling star
That shines each night from afar

And wider than the longest arms spread apart
That is how much a father's love is in your heart

2019

MARY MARTINA DOCKTER

SPECIAL DELIVERY

Because you are so special
With your tiny hands and feet
Our lives will be blessed full
On your birthday when we meet

But until that glorious day
Please stay warm until we see
The most precious gift heaven's way
A new baby by a stork's delivery

2012

AMAZING

Have you discovered your hands my little one
Those fingers can go this way and that way
They swirl and twirl and can also sway
No wonder you just stare, hands are lots of fun

Have you discovered your feet my little one
Those toes wiggle and jiggle and just stay
They go this way and that way and obey
No wonder you really care, feet are lots of fun

You discovered your hands and feet my little one
Those fingers and toes go this way and that way
They twirl and swirl, jiggle and wiggle at play
No wonder you're amazed, they are lots of fun

2012

TICKLE, TICKLE TOOTSIES

Tickle, tickle tootsies,
Ten in a row.

Tickle, tickle tootsies,
To bed they won't go.

The first little tootsie tries to hide,
But the other little tootsies are by his side.

The second little tootsie wishes to play,
But the other little tootsies say no way.

The third little tootsie wants something to eat,
But the other little tootsies have brushed their feet.

The fourth little tootsie starts to sing a song,
But the other little tootsies won't sing along.

The fifth little tootsie hopes to stay up late,
But the other little tootsies don't want to wait.

The sixth little tootsie a drink of water he tries,
But the other little tootsies only hear his cries.

The seventh little tootsie decides to be good,
But the other little tootsies won't do what they should.

The eighth little tootsie plans to run away,
But the other little tootsies make him stay.

The ninth little tootsie asks for a book read,
Why the other little tootsies agree, "yes" they said.

The tenth little tootsie finally goes to sleep,
And the other little tootsies fall asleep without a peep.

Tickle, tickle tootsies,
Ten in a row.

Tickle, tickle tootsies,
To bed they will go.

2013

MARY MARTINA DOCKTER

SWEET FEET

Wiggling, jiggling, wiggling toes
Splashing, laughing, splashing goes
When they jump in puddles, it takes away woes
Wiggling, jiggling, wiggling toes

Jiggling, wiggling, jiggling feet
Dancing, prancing, dancing beat
When they stomp to the music, it's so sweet
Jiggling, wiggling, jiggling feet

2012

THREE GRANDSONS

Three grandsons, three grandsons
See how they've grown, see how they've grown
They all cuddled and cooed and crawled with blithe
And learned how to walk by not falling from strife
Did you ever see so much joy in your life
As three grandsons, three grandsons

2010

FLUSH IT TO THE FISH

Flush it! Flush it!
That is the way.

We begin,
Each and every day.

Flush it! Flush it!
Do you want to know?

When you flush,
Where the flush goes.

Flush it! Flush it!
So every boy and girl.

Too big for diapers,
Can see the water twirl.

Flush it! Flush it!
The water goes around.

Where it goes,
Why it flows into fish town.

Flush it! Flush it!
You can do your part.

Making sure,
Your #1 or #2 departs.

Flush it! Flush it!
If feeding them is your wish.

Watch it swirl,
As you flush it to the fish.

2012

MARY MARTINA DOCKTER

RULES ARE THE RULES

Now, listen to me, listen to see.
No need to pout what it's about.
Life is just a matter of this trust.
For the rules are the rules in tools.

By being the best way in the day.
No matter win lose it's to choose.
How you react no matter the fact.
For the rules are the rules in tools.

It's time for bed you sleepy head.
So, brush your teeth, underneath.
To keep pearly whites do it right.
For the rules are the rules in tools.

And within a day and night's stay.
A parent's there because they care.
Respect for them, maturity begins.
For the rules are the rules in tools.

2021

WATCHING IS HELPING

When you're just three,
And you want to also see.

But you think you need to help,
You wish to be a big boy yourself.

The one thing you can do,
When, you're three, too.

Is be with your dad and just watch when,
By watching you are helping him.

When you're just five,
And you want to also try.

But there are things you cannot touch,
Little girls can get hurt too much.

The one thing you can do,
When, you're five, too.

Is be with your mom and just watch when,
By watching you are helping then.

When you wish to show,
And your parents they do know.

That you just want to help,
You want to be a big boy or girl yourself.

MARY MARTINA DOCKTER

The one thing you must agree,
No matter how young or old you may be.

Is if you really want to help out,
Watching is helping is what it's about.

2011

WATCHING IS GROWING

When you're laying in your crib,
With your rattle and your bib,
And mommy's there all the while,
Watching is growing, learning how to smile.

When you're staying on your blanket,
Rolling from side to side trying to make it,
And daddy's there to help you over,
Watching is growing, learning how to roll-over.

When you're no longer content on the ground,
Pulling up on things all around,
And mommy's there to give a helping hand,
Watching is growing, learning how to stand.

When you're about to take a step,
But still a little wobbly, wobbly, yet,
And daddy's there with "come to me," talk,
Watching is growing, learning how to walk.

When you're in your mommy's arms,
Showing off with all your charm,
And mommy's hand starts flying high,
Watching is growing, learning how to wave bye, bye.

When you're in your daddy's arms,
Still showing off with all your charm,
And daddy knows mommy will be missed,
Watching is growing, learning how to blow a kiss.

When you're bigger and want to go fast at play,
Because with some toys you just sit there and stay,
And mommy's there to watch you have fun,
Watching is growing, learning how to run.

When you're playing outside in the yard,
With a big, red ball on your guard,
And daddy's there to help you and show,
Watching is growing, learning how to throw.

When you're with other children for the day,
Having fun being able to play,
And mommy and daddy love you because they care,
Watching is growing, learning how to share.

2012

WATCHING IS LEARNING

A proud, new father holds his son so very dear,
Then gently lays him in the crib to be near.

The infant son's bed, his love surrounds,
As music plays and shapes go around.

A proud, new father leans forward and softly whispers to his son,
"Watching is learning," your world has begun.

A proud father can hardly believe how his son grew,
For soon is your birthday and you'll be turning two.

You've cooed and crawled and can walk around,
And your favorite shoes to wear are your dad's pair you have found.

A proud father is admired and adored by his son,
"Watching is learning," now you can run.

A proud father today shares with you his pride,
For his son is now older and going to be five.

He holds your hand and sits you on the ground,
As he starts to hammer, it makes a loud sound.

A proud father displays each and every tool,
"Watching is learning," is the golden rule.

A proud father and son go fishing at the lake,
For you love to explore nature now that you are eight.

MARY MARTINA DOCKTER

A net's in your hand and your feet are in the pond,
Your favorite place to be is with dad all day long.

A proud father is patient and shows you how to cast a line,
"Watching is learning," you'll be a pro in no time.

A proud father hardly knows where to begin,
For his son is now bigger and going to be ten.

You help your dad do chores around the home,
By this time you'll be doing some on your own.

A proud father keeps saying these words to his son,
"Watching is learning," growing up will soon come.

A proud father takes notice, his son's independent self,
For you are much older and bolder at twelve.

While riding your bike to school and back,
You look both ways and that is a fact.

A proud father each day does the best that he can,
"Watching is learning," you're becoming a young man.

A proud father prays when his son is in his teens,
For you think you are older but you are only sixteen.

Your friends are fun to have around,
But a father's love won't let you down.

A proud father hands over the keys to the car,
"Watching is learning," for soon you'll go far.

A proud father applauds his son accepts his diploma scene,
For time flies by so fast, you are now eighteen.

Your bright colored cap is thrown into the air,
A son believes in his heart his dad does care.

A proud father through the years has seen his son grow,
"Watching is learning," for now his son knows.

A proud father attends your college graduation, too,
For his son is now an adult at the age of twenty-two.

The day has come to put aside school books,
So you can find a good job and go to work.

A proud father has done the best that he can,
"Watching is learning," you're now a grown man.

A proud, new father holds his child so very dear,
For his life is complete now that you are here.

He gently lays you in the crib, his love surrounds,
As music plays and shapes go around.

A proud, new father leans forward and softly whispers to his daughter,
"Watching is learning," is my gift to you from your grandfather.

2011

                                        MARY MARTINA DOCKTER

WATCHING IS KNOWING

My little one, sweet little one, my little one on my knee,
Let's play a game, a game of what you see,
A game that's all about you, so you will get to know,
The different parts of your body by pointing I will show.

Your nose, your nose, your tiny, little nose,
As I point to your nose, your cute, button nose,
Watch me closely as I point to your nose to show,
So you can point to your nose too, by watching you will know.

Your eyes, your eyes, your big, beautiful eyes,
As I point to your eyes for soon you will surely try,
Watch me closely as I point to your eyes to show,
So you can point to your eyes too, by watching you will know.

Your ears, your ears, your special, little ears,
As I point to your ears, your ears that are very near,
Watch me closely as I point to your ears to show,
So you can point to your ears too, by watching you will know.

Your chin, your chin, your strong, little chin,
As I point to your chin for soon you will too, begin,
Watch me closely as I point to your chin to show,
So you can point to your chin too, by watching you will know.

Your lips, your lips, your red, little lips,
As I point to your lips, your lips you use to sip,
Watch me closely as I point to your lips to show,
So you can point to your lips too, by watching you will know.

Your head, your head, the top of your head,
As I point to your head, the hair on the top of your head,
Watch me closely as I point to your head to show,
So you can point to your head too, by watching you will know.

Your hands, your hands, your joyful, little hands,
As I point to your hands for soon you will understand,
Watch me closely as I point to your hands to show,
So you can point to your hands too, by watching you will know.

Your toes, your toes, your wiggly, little toes,
As I point to your toes, you wiggle your toes so,
Watch me closely as I point to your toes to show,
So you can point to your toes too, by watching you will know.

Your belly button, your belly button, your silly, little belly button,
As I point to your belly button, your belly button is really something,
Watch me closely as I point to your belly button to show,
So you can point to your belly button too, by watching you will know.

My little one, sweet little one, my little one on my knee,
You played a game with me, a game of what you see,
A game in watching is knowing that is what we do,
The different parts of your body, the game called you.

2012

   MARY MARTINA DOCKTER

BEYOND THE SIDEWALK

Where the sidewalk ends
There life will begin
For adventures are found
When you step down
So one must take that step
And then not regret
Because life begins when
The sidewalk ends

2012

AUTUMN GOLD

Bright colored hues do magically adorn them.

When leaves in the trees become nature's gems.

As they blow in the wind with shimmer of light.

They are jewels of the changing landscape sight.

This blessed treasured season is for all to behold.

For, we're enriched with beauty in autumn gold.

2012

CLIMBING TREE

Of all the trees you see in the forest around.

There's but a few good for climb I've found.

Some are too short and not worth your time.

While others are too tall and a fall is a crime.

The best would be straight, liken a ruler stick.

And branches used as steps on a ladder quick.

To get to the top so to take in all that you see.

When finding the right one, for climbing tree.

2022

SACRED SIMPLICITY

In living a soul does dwell
Similar to the existence of me
But none lives so simply well
As the sacred life of a tree

Growing, flowing, above
From nature's alluring dress
Wearing each leaf with love
In Spring's fashions best

A tree's limbs of shade
They say across many lands
Keeps Summer's heat obeyed
On a child's lemonade stand

Its world soon must change
Verd clothed nature's mother
A cold-spell soon to rearrange
Autumn leaves to Fall colors

For then forgotten beauty
Will forever be blown and lost
But blooming be hidden merely
By the veil of Winter's frost

In living a soul does dwell
Similar to the existence of me
But none lives so simply well
As the sacred life of a tree

2004

MARY MARTINA DOCKTER

KALEIDOSCOPE

Colors of life to see
Surround me
Take a peek
Within its sphere
Turn the world around
And around
Magical images
Do appear
Dancing
Colors of life
Come alive
Transforming
Digits of trees
Summer's leaves
Snowflakes
Winter's sneeze
Icicles
Bicycles
Different shapes
Life, makes
Whimsical hues
Imagination's clue
Red and orange
Blue, green
Take a peek
Colors of life to see
Surround me

2009

IF I COULD FLY

If I could fly, I think I would like to be
An eagle of radiant beauty and majesty
With wings that spread across this land
And glide on air in a commanding stand
My eyes like sharpen knives will pierce
In the sky I'll capture prey as I'm fierce
But alone, my flight of silence does cry
I am an eagle yes an eagle, if I could fly

2021

DREAM'S SCHEME

Night time comes before your eyes.
And you're sound asleep before you realize.
The day still lingers within your head.
But will play like a play in your head instead.

What is your wish when you're awake?
So just lie in bed and your head will then take.
Those wishes the day tells you be gone.
But the night won't say what you wish is wrong.

Do you dream of flying, way up there?
Is that your big wish, you can fly up in the air.
And glide over your house as in flight.
And be able to look down without any fright.

If that is your wish, then you are like me.
Because I dream of that often, flying you see.
I maybe awake in the day so it may seem.
As I wait for the night and its dream's scheme.

2021

FEATHER SERPENT

How to train a dragon!

The day's cumulus sky was one big rain cloud.
Good weather to sneak up on a dragon.
And that's exactly, the plan.
The young lad confident detects his pocket.
For, there he hides a secret weapon.

Wearing a disguise, he is well camouflaged.
Liken as a chameleon, becomes the mountain rock.
With steadfast determination, he reaches the crest.
The stripling lad assured, checks his pocket.
For, there lies the secret weapon.

The smell of sulfur becomes almost unbearable.
He crawls closer and closer to the dragon's portal cave.
There, a callow boy slowly stands tall.
The chevalier lad prepared scopes into his pocket.
For, there he tries the secret weapon.

The dormant incubus is caught by surprise.
When, a feather tickles this serpent under its nostrils.
And a gallant youth takes hold for a ride.
The clever thinking lad pulls hope from his pocket.
For, there he flies with his secret weapon.

2010

RUN WITH THE WIND

Spread the arms like wings of a bird.
And close your eyes not saying a word.
Feel the gentle wind within your hair.
It caresses your face nothing compares.
Then run with the wind to reach a height.
As you pretend to soar and take flight.

2021

FLY BY

Look at the sky
The morning sky
What may fly by
Before your eyes

A beautiful, colorful butterfly
A ladybug's polka dot dye
A bumble bee's pollinating try
A child's kite flying high
A plane flies across the sky

Look at the sky
The night sky
What may fly by
Before your eyes

A swooping bat flapping by
A shooting star falls to die
A man on the moon waves hi
A lightning bug's fire fly
A fireworks display up high

Look at the sky
The wonderful sky
What may fly by
Before your eyes

2012

MARY MARTINA DOCKTER

FLIGHT OF A KITE

Hold on, tiny fingers, to this delight.
Don't let go it might go out of sight.
It flies in the air with it your dreams.
And it floats without a care it seems

Dancing through the clouds it plays.
With a tug or with a release it obeys.
As the string, gives it life in a breeze.
Then be captured in branches of trees.

And it floats without a care it seems.
It flies in the air with it your dreams.
Don't let go, it might go out of sight.
Hold on, tiny fingers, to this, delight.

2022

WHIMSICAL WIND

Let's play outside and see what is there.
Maybe we'll discover a friend in the air.
It's one that comes and goes as it please.
And, even when it is there, not one sees.

This friend nearby, will be by your side.
A brisk walk in the forest, it will, abide.
When, trees wave, hello, with the leaves.
As they are thankful for the cool breeze.

A sauntering brook's also taking a stroll.
For both of you are adrift along the knoll.
With the wind at your back it helps along.
It keeps you on the journey going strong.

And, when, you meet the end of the road.
A friend will be waiting, to bear the load.
As you turn around and start it over again.
It will be there, mystical, whimsical wind.

2021

HALCYON DAYS

(Nostalgic Ways)

Bare feet scamper out the back door.
So toes, like little piglets can play in the grass.
And one runs through field of clover.
Do remember the days, happier times in the past.

And fly with a net to catch a butterfly.
With each swish of the hand, a question is asked.
When it, lands on a finger and not fly.
Do remember the days, happier times in the past.

One wades, knee-deep, a nearby pond.
And like an acrobat glides in air to make a splash.
A circus is in mind, a future beyond.
Do remember the days, happier times in the past.

And climb a vast tree to reach the stars.
Imagination controls a spaceship that won't crash.
Hold tight to reach the top one goes far.
Do remember the days, happier times in the past.

Bare feet scamper out the back door.
So toes, like little piglets can play in the grass.
And one runs through field of clover.
Do remember the days, happier times in the past.

2009

CHILDHOOD DAYS

Remember when days were filled with fun
The morning to arise by adventures begun
Friends gather and quarrel at games played
Even one out voted meant everyone stayed

Remember when a creek is there to explore
By the flowing of ice cold water to its shore
And wade through the rocks under our feet
Catch by a minnow or a crawdaddy's defeat

Remember when nights meant time to hide
Flashlights resemble fireflies in seek to find
For bedtime belies a child's end for the day
Dreams to continue children's gift of replay

Remember when days would last for years
And monsters in closets make believe fears
To live in each moment is childhood ways
With the art of play during childhood days

2004

COTTON CANDY SKY

Swirls and twirls of sugary puffs.
Way up looks like a child's muff.
It is white and soft to your touch.
But, it is not close to reach much.

A circus concession is displayed.
Clouds have become sweets made.
When, they float up in the air high.
It's then we see a cotton candy sky.

2021

BEWITCHING

Listen! Can you hear the wind singing.
As it plays a melody through the trees.
For the joyful leaves dance it is bringing.
It's a song for all children, in a breeze.

Vision! Close your eyes and feel a glee.
When, it tangles your hair into a mess.
And playing a tug a war, you cannot see.
Then it is like playing a game of chess.

Arisen! It's in the sunlight of a new day.
As it carries warmth, felt on your face.
For no one know when it comes or stays.
Bewitching air appears without a trace.

2022

MARY MARTINA DOCKTER

JUST A ROCK'N

When life is at a fast pace,
And it seems you're in a rat race.
Do you need to be in first place?
Then think, slow down to a safe haste,
Take the time to be just a rock'n.

Sit still and clear your mind,
Rock back and forth and you'll find.
Family and friends, they are so kind!
And together they're there to unwind,
Make the time to be just a talk'n.

Cars pass by and they wave at you,
You're on the front porch nothing to do.
But rock back and forth, if they only knew!
At peace with yourself and with those who,
Take the time to be just a honk'n.

When life is at a fast pace,
And it seems you're in a rat race.
Do you need to be in first place?
Then think, slow down to a safe haste,
Make the time to be just a rock'n.

2011

KIDS AND KATS

So you think you're the boss, the big cheese.
The owner of a cat or a parent that over sees.
For, the joke is on you, if you think that way.
Because cats and kids have the one final say.
Oh they let you believe that you're in charge.
With their cute faces, and eyes that are large.
But in the end we know the truth will be told.
So if you want to be the boss a puppy is sold.

2012

LIFT THEM UP

As you look down at your children at your feet.
Wide eyed and trusting arms, reach out to greet.
For you're the only one, they truly depend upon.
A mother or father is the heart, a future beyond.
Let not a day go by, this precious gift unopened.
Your love must always be there, they are hoping.
Security reaches out to them when they are pups.
So with caring eyes and loving arms lift them up.

2012

EVERY BREATH I WAKE

I'm up in the morning, break of dawn.
I stretch my arms and give out a yawn.
And greet the day with a grateful smile.
As I breathe the sweet air, I am a child.

Of this vast universe here on this earth.
There's much to be thankful for in birth.
I won't take for granted, this day's sake.
And each day, with every breath I wake.

2022

SUNRISE

Each day opens with eyes as sunrise
Upon this time life's garden to arise
A morning tide's quilt set aside near
It's coverlet a safe keeping from fear
Wake now and behold all that is new
Evergreen refreshed, yesterday grew
As golden rays rise, celebrate the sun
Good day to you, the day, has begun

2003

MY HAPPY PLACE

My favorite place
Is my, smile
My happy face!

So in its place
My sadness awhile
Will be erased.

My favorite place
Is my, smile
My happy face!

2012

MARY MARTINA DOCKTER

IT'S A PONDER FULL LIFE

(It's a Wonderful Life)

The peaceful night sleeps till dawn.
As the morning sun rises with yawn.
Upon a beautiful place when, awake.
For it's a wondrous day within a lake.

When all begin to stir open their eyes.
A new day has risen for life will arise.
And hear the music their calling make.
For it's a wondrous day within a lake.

Fish begin to swim and jump for prey.
As insects fly above then land to stay.
On top the cool water is their mistake.
For it's a wondrous day within a lake.

Then ducks and geese splash around.
And in the reeds frogs call the sound.
It's a, ponder full life, nature makes.
For it's a wondrous day within a lake.

2011

PEACEFUL PLACES

Peaceful places
Are friendly faces
Those quiet days
Be replayed
Sit and ponder
And go be yonder
By looking back
When relaxed
Summer flies by
Like the sky
The clouds above
Are pictures of
And with the night
You point in sight
At the stars
By gazing far
Then winter sings
For it can bring
Snow falling down
An angel found
And white on your face
Will be no trace
Of stress around
When lying down
So sit and rock
For thoughts have brought
You together again
Now and then
And live from there
Without a care
One's weathered face
A peaceful place

2011

MARY MARTINA DOCKTER

ELEMENTARY

ABC
Look at me
You can be
When you believe

ABC
Eyes on me
You can be
When you can read

2011

FUNDAMENTAL

Eyes wide open, questions spoken, yearning to learn
Pencils writing, lessons reciting, taking turns
Students reading, minds retrieving, every word
Full of wonder, when you're younger, like a bird
Imagination's soaring, when exploring, crossing the bridge
Kindergarten's over, 1" grade is older, just a smidge
And 5th grade today, is harder but also play, and knowledge
Elementary is the tool, there's middle school, high school and college

2017

MARY MARTINA DOCKTER

READ TO GROW

Feed your mind the written word,
For it hungers to know and grow!

2011

DAISY DAYS

May your day be like a flower!
Joyfully dancing in sunshine,
Boyishly standing in the rain,
Playfully blowing in the wind,
Magically growing in a Daisy,
In the garden of everyday life!

2012

THE BEST DAY

The sun shines on my face
All my troubles are erased
With a blue sky I do eye
A butterfly and bird fly by
There's a skip to my walk
A cheerful smile as I talk
For life is happy and clever
When, it's the best day ever

2012

THINK HAPPY THOUGHTS

Kittens and puppies
Dolphins and guppies
A warm summer breeze
Leaves dancing in trees
Ice-cold lemon-aide
The coolness of shade
And splashing along
Thru a creek or pond
A cold winter freeze
So Santa Claus sees
All children at pray
For Christmas day
Then melting snow
On tongue and nose
And holding hands
Of family and friends
Are those I sought
My happy thoughts

2011

BE LIKE THE TURTLE

Enter a living space with a cautious face
And be slow to enquire a place with trial
Keep treasures safe within a self's place
So life's shell will tow wherever you go
And wherever you are home is never far

2009

LET LADYBUGS COME

Just lay in the grass
And keep perfectly still
No need hunt for them a task
When they come by their free will

2009

MARY MARTINA DOCKTER

BE STILL

Be still
Be real
Be true
Be you
Be near
Be here
Be real
Be still

2012

JUST BE YOU

Be just who you are
Be like a shooting star
Be just uniquely true
BE JUST YOU!

2011

MARY MARTINA DOCKTER

AN EAR FULL

Dreams are angels,
Whispering in your ears,
Never stop listening,
Always keep believing!

2020

LULLABY SEA

Within a deep sleep one will float into the sea.
Into the sea a day will end and the night to be.
And one's dreams will be the sail on this ship.
When, one closes their eyes will begin this trip.

With a wink of an eye one prepares to aboard.
As hands will discover a night's yawn, reward.
And soon to begin is this vision in one's head.
To be on this voyage one must be in their bed.

With a blink of an eye the vessel is on its way.
Thru a wave of tears and twinkling stars obey.
And guide one through this journey the night.
It keeps one safe in the dark until the daylight.

With a nod of one's head one has made it thru.
As one sails through the night beyond the blue.
For the day's forgotten and all worries set free.
When, one closes their eyes on the Lullaby Sea.

2009

SUNSET

Each night closes with eyes as sunset
Upon this time life is due somnolence
An evening tide's quilt caresses near
It's coverlet, a safe keeping from fear
Sleep now and behold all that's done
Garden bedded, tomorrow has begun
Golden rays lower, darkness the win
Good night to you, the night to begin

2003

GOODNIGHT KISSES

Goodnight kisses
In your bed

Goodnight kisses
Sleepyhead

Goodnight kisses
Dreams to be

Goodnight kisses
Read to me

Goodnight kisses
With a book

Goodnight kisses
Take a look

Goodnight kisses
Time we share

Goodnight kisses
A teddy bear

Goodnight kisses
Off the light

Goodnight kisses
Nighty-night

2013

MARY MARTINA DOCKTER

CHAPTER TWO

SIBLING STORIES

SIBLING STORIES

There once was a sister and brother you see.
As this sister and brother is a family of bees.
They lived with their parents in the beehive.
For it's there their sibling stories come alive.
So, come lie in your bed, a favorite toy near.
And, tucked in with blankets no more, fears.
Then mommy or daddy reads to you tonight.
And soon you're asleep dreaming goodnight

2021

BEE BEAUTIFUL

Honey and Bumble Bee,
They are sister and brother we.

But even though they are family,
Each one is a different kind of bee.

Honey a honeybee is smaller with a fuzzy middle,
Her abdomen is sleek and her thin wings wiggle.

She can only sting once if given the chance,
But not any honeybee males, they can only dance.

Honey Bee has a very special talent, too,
Mrs. Mother Bee and Honey Bee produce honey for you.

Bumble a bumblebee is fat with a thick furry body,
He is yellow, orange and or black and has dense wings you see.

Bumblebees can sting many times not just the one chance,
But only female bumblebees, so Mr. Father Bee
and Bumble Bee can only dance.

And together they are different but the same,
Honey a honeybee and Bumble a bumblebee by name.

Because Honey and Bumble Bee,
They are sister and brother we.

But even though they are family,
Each one is a different kind of bee.

And that is why being different means you're being suitable,
By being yourself one will always **Bee Beautiful.**

2015

MARY MARTINA DOCKTER

BEE GROWING

Honey and Bumble Bee,
They are sister and brother, you see.

And together they like to compare,
If sister bee or brother bee has grown, is the dare.

Mrs. Mother Bee has a very special ruler for the task,
And Honey Bee and Bumble Bee, they just need to ask.

Buzz, buzz, buzz, "Can we flutter under the ruler today?"
Buzz, buzz and buzz, "Why yes, Honey and Bumble, you may."

So Honey Bee flies to stay still by hovering near the wall,
Then Mrs. Mother Bee holds the ruler to show her how tall.

She uses a blue pen to document Honey Bee's height,
And it doesn't hurt a bit even though you think it might.

So next it is Bumble Bee's turn to fly tall and straight,
And Mrs. Mother Bee uses a red pen this time to make.

A mark on the wall to document how tall he has grown,
Because blue is for Honey Bee and red is for Bumble Bee known.

For Mrs. Mother Bee has a very special ruler for the task,
And Honey Bee and Bumble Bee, they just need to ask.

Buzz, buzz, buzz, "Who grew the most," they both would say?
Buzz, buzz and buzz, "Who was the winner today?"

But Mrs. Mother Bee smiles and buzzes,
"You both grew about the same,"
"Honey Bee and Bumble Bee," saying both their names.

Because Honey and Bumble Bee,
They are sister and brother, you see.

And together they like to compare the showing,
If sister bee or brother bee, would Bee Growing.

2014

MARY MARTINA DOCKTER

BEE YOU, BEE ME

Honey and Bumble Bee,
They're each unique as a bee can be.

Honey Bee is the older sister of the two,
She loves to be with her friends and the color blue.

Bumble Bee is the younger brother, who likes the color red,
He likes to be with friends but sometimes
he'd rather be alone instead.

Honey Bee always wants to invite her friends over,
They buzz, buzz, and buzz, gossiping while flying over clover.

Bumble Bee would rather sit quietly while
playing cars with his wings,
He vroom, vroom and vrooms,
mimicking the sound a car's engine would bring.

Honey Bee collecting nectar prefers flowers that are blue,
Because blue is her favorite color with anything to do.

Bumble Bee collecting nectar prefers a different color instead,
A flower that is bright and bold. A flower that is red.

So Honey and Bumble Bee,
They're each unique as a bee can be.

Honey Bee is the older sister of the two,
She loves to be with her friends and the color blue.

Bumble Bee is the younger brother, who likes the color red,
He likes to be with friends but sometimes
he'd rather be alone instead.

But Honey Bee and Bumble Bee they both will agree,
You can Bee You, and I can Bee Me.

2014

   MARY MARTINA DOCKTER

BEE THANKFUL

Honey and Bumble Bee,
They live in a hive, high in a tree.

With Father Bee, Mother Bee, sister and brother,
They're a family of bees, together with each other.

Father Bee is big and strong and takes good care,
He takes good care of Mother Bee, sister and brother living there.

And Honey Bee and Bumble Bee like to say,
"Father Bee is the best father in the world, hooray."

Mother Bee is beautiful and strong and takes good care,
She takes good care of Father Bee, sister and brother living there.

And Honey Bee and Bumble Bee like to say,
"Mother Bee is the best mother in the world, hooray."

Because Honey and Bumble Bee,
They live in a hive, high in a tree.

With Father Bee, Mother Bee, sister and brother,
They're a family of bees, together with each other.

For Honey Bee and Bumble Bee are always giving tours,
To show off their beehive just like you with yours.

And Honey Bee and Bumble Bee like to say,
"Their beehive is the best home in the world, hooray."

Because Honey and Bumble Bee,
They live in a hive, high in a tree.

And together they're a family of bees very grateful,
They have their home and each other to Bee Thankful.

2014

 MARY MARTINA DOCKTER

BEE KNOWING

Honey and Bumble Bee,
They are sister and brother, you see.

And together as a family,
They go to the Bee Hive Library.

Honey Bee and Bumble Bee enjoy going there,
When they're at the Bee Hive Library nothing can compare.

Because so many books are there for them to read,
Honey Bee and Bumble Bee wish they
could pick more than just three.

Honey Bee likes books about ballerinas, fairies and princesses,
And can imagine being rescued by a handsome bee prince when.

Bumble Bee likes books about super heroes, spaceships and cars,
And can imagine being an astronaut in a spaceship travelling far.

But Honey Bee and Bumble Bee must decide on what books to take,
It's a tough decision when they can only
pick three for goodness sake.

Because so many books are there for them to read,
And then finally decide on which books should be the three.

Honey and Bumble Bee,
They are sister and brother, you see.

And together as a family,
They go to the Bee Hive Library.

Honey Bee and Bumble Bee enjoy going there,
When they're at the Bee Hive Library nothing can compare.

Because so many books are there for one's imagination growing,
Honey Bee and Bumble Bee read to Bee Knowing.

2014

 MARY MARTINA DOCKTER

BEE YOUR BEST

Honey and Bumble Bee,
They both go to Bee School happily.

Where, Bumble Bee is in first grade with many of his friends,
And Honey Bee is in an upper grade at
the school where they attend.

Honey Bee and Bumble Bee rise early everyday,
They eat a good breakfast of honey to get them on their way.

And together they fly to school before the bell rings,
So they can get in line with their classmates as their teacher sings.

"Buzz, buzz, buzz," School is about to begin,
"Buzz, buzz, buzz," Is every little bee here to come in?

And together they fly into school as the bell rings,
So they can learn with their classmates as their teacher sings.

"Buzz, buzz, buzz," The lesson for today,
"Buzz, buzz, buzz," Be your best everyday.

Because Honey Bee and Bumble Bee try very hard at school,
To do the best work they can do and that is the only rule.

As long as you do your best it doesn't matter then,
If another bee does even better, by doing your best you still win.

For Honey and Bumble Bee.
They both go to Bee School happily.

Where, Honey Bee and Bumble Bee try very hard with the rest,
As they learn with their classmates, Bee Your Best.

2014

                    MARY MARTINA DOCKTER

BEE ALL YOU CAN BEE

Honey and Bumble Bee,
They like flying to the highest tree.

Because Honey Bee believes she's the fastest one,
While Bumble Bee disagrees, he's already won.

But no one is the winner if all you do is talk,
Just because you buzz you've won doesn't mean squat.

So father and mother bee decide to put on a race,
To see who is the fastest to the tree, all doubts will be erased.

For Honey and Bumble Bee are eager to know,
Which bee is the fastest, on your mark, get set, go.

At first it looks like Honey Bee is certain to win,
But Bumble Bee gives it his all they're neck and neck again.

They're wings are flapping faster about 230 beats per second,
No bee can withstand this pressure they're bound to quit I recon.

But Honey and Bumble Bee are determine, to finish the race,
To see who is the fastest to the tree, all doubts will be erased.

Because Honey Bee likes to proclaim she is the fastest one,
While Bumble Bee believes he's already won.

So when the race is almost over and the tree is in sight,
Both bees are announced the winner, for a tie was their delight.

For Honey and Bumble Bee,
They like flying to the highest tree.

Only now they are sure to agree,
As both are winners, Bee all you can Bee.

2015

　　　　　　　MARY MARTINA DOCKTER

BEE A STAR

Honey and Bumble Bee,
They like to pretend who they want to be.

By imagining themselves as they get older,
When trying on costumes to be pretty or bolder.

Honey Bee likes to wear a beautiful dress,
She imagines herself an actress above the rest.

With her frilly clothes she can twirl and dance around,
When imagining herself performing in her town.

Bumble Bee likes to fly around wearing a cape,
He imagines himself catching a bad bee trying to escape.

With his flowing cape he can jump and prance around,
When imagining himself a superhero in his town.

Honey and Bumble Bee,
They like to pretend who they want to be.

By imagining themselves as they get older,
When trying on costumes to be pretty or bolder.

Because it is fun to imagine what it will be like,
When a little bee grows up and is no longer a tiny tike.

But Father Bee and Mother Bee know already who they are,
Honey Bee and Bumble will Bee A Star.

2015

BEE WISHFUL

Honey and Bumble Bee,
They wish upon a star and believe.

Their dreams are wishes to come true,
When, wishing upon a star like Honey and Bumble do.

Honey and Bumble Bee,
Lay quiet on the grass at night to see.

The many stars twinkling in the night sky,
When, wishing upon a star just like you and I.

Honey Bee searches for the brightest star at night,
For she knows the brightest star has the magical light.

Bumble Bee searches for the biggest star he sees,
Because he knows the biggest star has the magic he believes.

So Honey Bee and Bumble Bee pick out their very own star,
While they, lay quiet on the grass looking up into the night far.

They close their bug eyes as their wishes take flight,
Their dreams drift into the dark sky to greet a special star tonight.

When, they open their bug eyes they're so happy with glee,
Honey Bee's star is twinkling brighter and
Bumble Bee's star is bigger you see.

Because Honey and Bumble Bee,
Believe wishes do come true they agree.

When, wishing upon a star that is whimsical,
Just like Honey and Bumble, Bee Wishful.

2014

BEE COURAGEOUS

Honey and Bumble Bee,
They're sometimes afraid, you see.

When trying something new to them,
They hide behind their wings not knowing then.

Every little bee is sometimes afraid when trying something new,
But, not every little bee is aware of just what to do.

So Mrs. Mother Bee buzzed, "Trying
something new can be a game,"
Well, Honey Bee and Bumble Bee wanted Mother Bee to explain.

Buzz, buzz, buzz, "When trying something
new imagine being brave like a lion,"
Honey Bee and Bumble Bee thought this
was silly, without even trying.

Then one day when Honey and Bumble Bee
were afraid trying something new out,
They started to hide behind their wings and begin to pout.

Suddenly they remembered what Mother Bee had to say,
"Imagine being brave like a lion and not be afraid today."

Honey Bee and Bumble Bee roared like a lion,
Why, they were not afraid of something new
with this game they were trying.

Because every little bee is sometimes afraid
when trying something new,
But, not every little bee is aware of just what to do.

So instead of hiding behind your wings,
imagine being something outrageous,
Imagine becoming a lion to conquer your fears and Bee Courageous.

2014

BEE DARING

Honey and Bumble Bee,
They like to explore and see.

The many exciting places outside their home,
When, Honey Bee and Bumble Bee decide to roam.

Mrs. Mother Bee packs them a nutritious snack,
For, they don't know exactly when they'll get back.

And together Honey and Bumble Bee are off to explore,
When, Honey Bee and Bumble Bee go out their front door.

Mr. Father Bee stays close by but he doesn't want to be seen,
For, he wants them to be brave, if you know what I mean.

And together Honey Bee and Bumble Bee are off to explore,
Discovering new and exciting places for an adventure.

They find a lovely field of clover filled with sweet nectar,
While, Mr. Father Bee quietly hovers nearby, wishing not to stir.

As they gather the flowers' nectar to take the prize home,
This will show their parents how brave they are to roam.

Because Honey and Bumble Bee,
They like to explore and see.

The many exciting places outside their home,
When, Honey Bee and Bumble Bee decide to roam.

And Mr. Father Bee and Mrs. Mother Bee will be there caring,
So Honey Bee and Bumble Bee can Bee Daring.

2015

BEE BUSY

Honey and Bumble Bee,
They're sometimes very bored, you see.

When they think they have nothing to do,
As they complain by buzzing, "BOO HOO."

So Mrs. Mother Bee comes flying in,
"Why don't you two go play outside, then."

But Honey Bee and Bumble Bee just look at each other,
"There's nothing to do inside or outside," they told their mother.

"Well," buzzed Mrs. Mother Bee, "I think I can fix that."
"There are plenty of chores I can think of." So
Honey Bee and Bumble Bee did scat.

They flew into their bedrooms not wanting to be caught,
With having to do chores, they both definitely did not.

Honey Bee and Bumble Bee buzzed to each other,
"Can I play in your room?" But they both
answered, "Not with this clutter."

"My room is a mess!" Honey Bee buzzed to her brother,
"So is mine," Bumble Bee buzzed. "Hey,
why don't we help each other?"

Honey Bee and Bumble Bee together picked up their toys,
They made it into a race to see who could be first girls or boys.

MARY MARTINA DOCKTER

And when they were done they had plenty of room to play,
So by keeping busy they were not bored today.

Because Honey and Bumble Bee,
They're sometimes very bored, you see.

When, they think they have nothing to do and in a tizzy,
Oh, but there is plenty to do, if you just Bee Busy.

2014

BEE SHARING

Honey and Bumble Bee,
They're sometimes very stingy, you see.

And do not want to share with each other,
Honey Bee sister and Bumble Bee brother.

"This is mine," they would buzz, buzz, buzz,
"This is mine and not yours," they would buzz because.

Honey and Bumble Bee,
They're sometimes very stingy, you see.

And do not want to share with each other,
Honey Bee sister and Bumble Bee brother.

So Mrs. Mother Bee puts away all their toys,
Buzzing," I know of some little bees who'd share these toys with joy."

"Did you know some little bees have nothing to play with?"
"I'm sure these toys of yours would make a great gift."

Honey Bee and Bumble Bee were very sorry that day,
They apologized to each other and buzzed,
"Let's share our toys, O.K."

MARY MARTINA DOCKTER

And not only did they share with each other,
Honey Bee and Bumble Bee each picked a toy to give to another.

Because Honey and Bumble Bee,
They are good little bees, you see.

For it is better to be bees, who are caring,
And not be stingy but, Bee Sharing.

2014

BEE GOOD

Honey and Bumble Bee,
They're sometimes not as good as they can be.

For Honey Bee likes to try on many clothes,
But, they never end up in the hamper, where dirty clothes, goes.

Bumble Bee likes to play with all of his toys,
But, they never end up in the toy box after
his playing has been deployed.

Honey Bee likes to buzz, buzz, buzz for hours on the phone,
But, she never thinks of others who want
to use the phone, also alone.

Bumble Bee likes to take a hot bath with his tiny duck,
But, he never thinks of others because he never cleans the tub up.

Honey Bee likes to fix a snack after being at school,
But, she never thinks of her brother who might be hungry too.

Bumble Bee likes to tease his sister until she cries,
But, he never thinks about how it feels until he realized.

It doesn't feel very good when his sister teases him,
And that is when they both decide to change their bad habits when.

Honey Bee who likes to try on many clothes,
Decided to put them in the hamper where dirty clothes, goes.

MARY MARTINA DOCKTER

Bumble Bee who likes to play with his toys on the floor,
Decided to put them in the toy box because
that is where they're stored.

Honey Bee who likes to buzz, buzz, buzz on the phone,
Decided not to talk for hours but let others also use the phone alone.

Bumble Bee who likes to take a hot bath with his tiny duck,
Decided he'd clean up after he is done so he scrubbed the tub up.

So Honey Bee fixed a snack after school for Bumble Bee too,
And together they decided not to tease each other till they're blue.

Then Honey and Bumble Bee understood,
It is better to Bee Good.

2014

BEE NICE

Honey and Bumble Bee,
Are sister and brother, you see.

And like many sisters and brothers,
They too, can be mean to each other.

Honey Bee teases her brother because he is so small,
She teases him by buzzing. "You're not growing at all."

"Buzz, buzz, buzz," she whispers in his ears,
"Buzz, buzz, buzz," she teases until he cries real tears.

Bumble Bee may be small but he gets his sister back,
He pokes her with his stinger when he is on the attack.

Poke, poke, poke, he pretends to give a sting,
Poke, poke, poke, he pokes her until she sings.

"Mom, mom, mom, Bumble Bee is touching me,"
While Bumble Bee cries, "But mom, mom,
mom, Honey Bee is teasing me."

Then Mrs. Mother Bee smiles and says,
"It doesn't feel good does it?"
"When, being teased or being poked," so she made them both, sit.

So Honey Bee and Bumble Bee sat quietly in time out,
They sat and sat and sat until they could figure it out.

That teasing a younger brother never gets you anywhere,
And poking an older sister only gets you in a chair.

Then Honey Bee and Bumble Bee apologized to each other,
For, Bumble Bee loves his sister and Honey Bee loves her brother.

Because Honey and Bumble Bee,
Are sister and brother, you see.

And they do not need to be told twice,
You're not to be mean but to Bee Nice.

2014

BEE SORRY

Honey and Bumble Bee,
They are sometimes not very nice, you see.

When, they forget about being polite,
As they say, mean things when they fight.

Because Honey and Bumble Bee,
They are sister and brother, you see.

And like many sisters and brothers,
They too, will disagree with each other.

Honey Bee is upset because Bumble Bee is always there,
And Bumble Bee is upset because Honey Bee won't share.

So Mrs. Mother Bee tells Honey and Bumble Bee to try,
Stop fighting for a minute and just listen to each other's cry.

Honey Bee calmly explains she only wants a little time alone,
Bumble Bee agrees for Honey Bee will share now that it is known.

Then, Honey Bee and Bumble Bee give each other hugs,
And say they are sorry because they want to be good bugs.

Honey and Bumble Bee,
They are sometimes not very nice, you see.

When, they forget about being polite,
As they say, mean things when they fight.

                    MARY MARTINA DOCKTER

Because Honey and Bumble Bee,
They are sister and brother, you see.

And like many sisters and brothers,
They too, will disagree with each other.

But Honey Bee and Bumble Bee discovered being gnarly,
Is not the polite thing to do, when, one should Bee Sorry.

2014

BEE HUMBLE

Honey and Bumble Bee,
Are sister and brother, you see.

And like many sisters and brothers,
They too, disagree with each other.

It is Honey Bee, who believes she is the best,
When getting the nectar from flowers at rest.

But Bumble Bee thinks he is the one,
Who gets the most nectar when, the job is done.

So Honey and Bumble Bee
They agree to have a competition to see.

Which bee, brings the most nectar to the bee hive,
Why surely this contest will be able to decide.

If Honey Bee is the bee, to win at this game,
Or is Bumble Bee the bee to put his sister to shame.

And away they flew buzzing and buzzing around,
As they collect the nectar from flowers they have found.

But Honey Bee soon realized Bumble Bee was being left behind,
Because he wasn't as fast as he thought he was in his own mind.

Then Honey Bee decided she would let her little brother win,
By secretly helping him, gather the nectar in.

The flower petals she would fly upon and come to rest,
As she helps collect the pollen on his body
so her brother could be the best.

And Honey and Bumble Bee
Like many sisters and brothers disagree.

But by letting the other win just like Bumble,
It is sometimes better to agree, to Bee Humble.

2014

BEE HELPFUL

Honey and Bumble Bee,
They're busy as busy can be.

"Buzz, buzz, buzz," they sing indoors,
"Buzz, buzz, buzz," while doing chores.

Honey Bee is helping by gathering unwanted pollen that is stashed,
She collects it on her wings then throws it in the trash.

Bumble Bee is helping by picking up his toys,
He picks up all the toys even girl toys with the boys.

And Mrs. Mother Bee is very thankful for their hard work,
By rewarding them with a treat because she knows just what it took.

Honey and Bumble Bee,
They're busy as busy can be.

"Buzz, buzz, buzz," they sing outdoors,
"Buzz, buzz, buzz," while doing chores.

Honey Bee is helping by gathering the nectar nearby,
She collects it on her wings as she flies, flies, flies.

Bumble Bee is helping by picking up more of his toys,
He picks up all the toys even girl toys with the boys.

And Mr. Father Bee is very thankful for their hard work,
By rewarding them with a treat because he knows just what it took.

MARY MARTINA DOCKTER

Honey and Bumble Bee,
They're busy as busy can be.

When doing chores is fun not dull,
Honey and Bumble can Bee Helpful.

2014

BEE SILLY

Honey and Bumble Bee,
They're sometimes too serious, you see.

And forget to have fun with each other,
Honey Bee sister and Bumble Bee brother.

So Mrs. Mother Bee suggests they should rhyme,
And stop being so serious and have a good time.

Honey Bee and Bumble Bee begin to sing a song,
"Buzz, buzz, buzz," they both sing along.

Then, Mrs. Mother Bee plays music so they can dance,
Wiggle, wiggle, wiggle, goes their bellies as they prance.

And together they sing and dance and have fun,
But Honey Bee sister and Bumble Bee brother are not done.

Because Mr. Father Bee wants to join in and say,
What kind of games Honey Bee and Bumble Bee should play?

So Mr. Father Bee suggests hide and find,
And stop being so serious and have a good time.

Seek, seek, seek, they look for each other,
Honey Bee sister and Bumble Bee brother.

Then, Mr. Father Bee plays music so they can dance,
Jiggle, jiggle, jiggle, goes their bellies as they prance.

And together they sing and dance and have fun,
Honey Bee, Bumble Bee, Father Bee, Mother Bee, everyone.

Because Honey and Bumble Bee,
They're sometimes too serious, you see.

And forget to have fun when being frilly,
So stop being serious and just Bee Silly.

2014

BEE TRUE TO YOURSELF

Honey and Bumble Bee,
Wish they could express accurately.

How they are feeling inside,
When, sometimes their feelings have lied.

"I want to be by myself today," Honey Bee moans,
But when friends are over it's hard to be alone.

So she pretends to be happy and smile,
Even though, she is crying inside all the while.

"I want to play with a friend," Bumble Bee admits,
But mother bee is too busy to commit.

So he pretends to be happy and smile,
Even though, he is crying inside all the while.

Then Honey and Bumble Bee,
Decide to convey their feelings accurately.

And Honey Bee tells her friends how she feels,
For they truly understand and say it's no big deal.

And Bumble Bee tells his mom he wishes to play,
With a friend and his mom says it's OK.

For it is better to keep your feelings off the shelf,
And express them and Bee True to Yourself.

2015

BEE SMILING

Honey and Bumble Bee,
They're not always flying happily.

Sometimes their mood is very grim,
They buzz around the hive without a grin.

But no bee wants to be around gloom bugs then,
When Honey and Bumble are being like them.

For they soon realize being alone together is no fun,
They don't want just each other to be the only one.

That will fly around and play today,
They better change their mood in a fast way.

So Honey and Bumble Bee,
They started flying happily.

As their mood is no longer grim,
They start buzzing around the hive with a grin.

And every bee wants to be around happy bugs then,
When Honey and Bumble are being like them.

Because Honey and Bumble Bee will bring,
Happiness when they Bee Smiling.

2014

BEE HAPPY

Honey and Bumble Bee,
They're unhappy as they can be.

Instead of smiling faces, they're wearing frowns,
Because Honey and Bumble are feeling down.

Today, they are unable to play outside,
It is wet and cold as the sun did hide.

And Honey Bee and Bumble Bee have nothing to do,
When, stuck in their beehive without a clue.

But Mrs. Mother Bee has a different plan,
For, there is plenty to do other than.

Honey and Bumble just playing outside,
When, it is just as fun to play inside.

Mrs. Mother Bee suggests, a game of hide and seek,
And before they knew it, they forgot to peek.

If the rain had stopped, and the sun was out,
"Yes, this is fun!" They both did shout.

Because today they are unable to play outside,
It is wet and cold as the sun did hide.

MARY MARTINA DOCKTER

And throughout the day there was plenty to do,
When, Honey Bee and Bumble Bee discovered the clue.

Instead of wearing frown faces, smiling faces they agree,
Why be sad, when Honey and Bumble can Bee Happy.

2014

BEE PATRIOTIC

Honey and Bumble Bee,
They're sitting on their father bee's knee.

Listening to his buzzing on how thankful he is free,
But Honey and Bumble just sit there quietly.

Until Honey Bee hovers in mid air and soon begins to shout,
"Why do we fly the bee flag, what's it all about?"

Bumble Bee nods his head and he agrees,
"Yes father, please tell us the story of our history."

The Revolutionary War between the wasps and bees began,
When, wasps across the ocean ruled over the bees in this new land.

For our forefathers were unable to collect any pollen,
Unless they gave the wasps a majority of what they hauled in.

So a band of minute bees gathered to defend what was theirs,
And not be taxed to death by wasps that didn't care.

And even though the wasps were bigger in number and in size,
The bees were able to defeat the enemy for liberty was their prize.

                    MARY MARTINA DOCKTER

To this day every bee is free just like the flower,
For that is why we fly the bee flag, for freedom's power.

So Honey and Bumble Bee,
While sitting on their father bee's knee.

Listening to his buzzing about their history's symbolic,
As they wave the bee flag to Bee Patriotic.

2015

BEE HEALTHY

Honey and Bumble Bee,
They're not always trying to be healthy.

Instead of exercise and plenty of sleep,
Watching TV and eating junk food is better they agree.

Honey's favorite snack is a bowl of chips,
And don't forget its sidekick, lots and lots of dip.

Bumble's favorite snack is a chocolate, candy bar,
He doesn't like caramel but lots and lots of peanuts by far.

And together they'll sit in front of the TV,
Not doing anything but munching and staring like zombies.

Until Mother Bee intervenes with some healthy snacks,
By replacing chips and candy with fruits and veggies they lack.

Then she turns off the TV and tells them to play outside,
Children should be flying around, not glued to the TV inside.

So Honey and Bumble Bee decide to give it a try,
They eat their healthy snacks and go outside to fly.

And together they have lots of fun playing in the yard,
Why getting exercise and eating healthy is not very hard.

MARY MARTINA DOCKTER

So when the day is done and it is time for bed,
They get plenty of sleep these sleepy heads.

For Honey and Bumble Bee,
They're now trying to Bee Healthy.

2014

BEE YOUNG AT HEART

Honey and Bumble Bee,
Believe parents don't play, they're too busy.

When Honey and Bumble are playing around,
They think they're the ones who invented this playground.

Honey is older and somewhat wiser of the two,
She believes in her heart that her parents haven't a clue.

On how to have fun and not be working all the time,
Even Bumble thinks parents not having fun is a crime.

But little do they know what having fun is all about,
For Honey and Bumble are soon to learn their parents have clout.

Because they have played since they were very young,
And having fun is for everyone.

Just because parents are older doesn't mean they can't play,
Why, Mr. and Mrs. Bee are playing even today.

Mr. Bee is on a tennis league hitting balls with his wings,
It is he who was first to use pollen that a flower brings.

Mrs. Bee likes to fly as fast as the wind,
It is she who was first to race with all of her friends.

Mr. Bee enjoys a good game of hide-n-seek,
It is he who plays with Honey and Bumble and tries to peek.

Mrs. Bee takes the time to play games when it rains,
It is she who plays with sister and brother and doesn't complain.

So when Honey and Bumble are playing around,
They no longer believe they invented this playground.

As they've become wiser from when they did start,
And believe when you're older you can still Bee Young at Heart.

2015

CHAPTER THREE

TAILTALES

TAIL TALES

They squeak they're meek these rodents that matter.

As they tell their stories of glory in a mousy chatter.

And from beginning to the end they'll use their tail.

Young and old, a message is told, by their fairytales.

2021

THE ABC MOUSE

In a very special school house,
There lives a very special school mouse.

This very special mouse goes to school during the day,
When, his fellow mouse friends just want to play.

But this very special mouse knows the
importance of being in school,
And that learning the one, two, three's of
the ABC's is the golden rule.

So while his many mouse friends scamper around and climb,
This very special mouse decides not to waste his time.

He sits in the front row in class and is ready to go,
To learn the one, two, three's of the ABC's he wants to know.

And with his tiny, mouse paw he traces the letter A,
The letter A is for apple, he and his classmates all say.

For this tiny mouse and his classmates all want to learn,
The ABC's of the alphabet, so each letter will take a turn.

The letter B is next in line you see,
The letter B is for buzzing, bumble bee.

The letter C is special and all that,
The letter C is for a cuddly cat.

The letter D prances from there to here,
When, the letter D is a dancing deer.

The letter E wants to be the one in front,
The letter E is an elegant elephant.

The letter F flies, flies in the sky,
The letter F flies like a firefly.

The letter G is great, great to note,
The letter G is a gracious, grateful goat.

The letter H is more than you will know,
The letter H is for a healthy, happy hippo.

The letter I is made of ice, who knew,
When, the letter I becomes an igloo.

The letter J looks like a hook but yet,
The letter J is a soaring jet.

The letter K always goes to great heights,
When, the letter K flies high like a kite.

The letter L just roars and lies around,
When, the letter L is a loud and lazy lion.

The letter M swings from tree to tree,
The letter M is a mischievous monkey.

The letter N becomes a place to rest,
The letter N is a home as a bird's nest.

The letter O is really quite awesome,
When, the letter O becomes a quiet opossum.

The letter P hasn't stop bowing since,
The letter P turned into a proper prince.

MARY MARTINA DOCKTER

The letter Q has the higher rank it seems.
When, the letter Q is the alphabet queen.

The letter R runs, runs when scat,
The letter R runs like a rascally rat.

The letter S coils so it can make,
The letter S becomes a slithering snake.

The letter T is tough and so much mightier,
When, the letter T transforms into a tiger.

The letter U is this unique fella,
The letter U is best known as an umbrella.

The letter V is very musical when,
The letter V plays like a violin.

The letter W welcomes all to know,
The letter W opens as a window.

The letter X is very unusual in this way,
The letter X is like an X-ray.

The letter Z is last but not least of all,
When, this very special mouse and classmates yell out Z for zebra.

Because in a very special school house,
There lives a very special school mouse.

For this very special mouse knows the
importance of going to school,
And that learning the one, two, three's of
the ABC's is the golden rule.

2012

THE BARNYARD MOUSE

There lives in the country a barnyard mouse,
Where, this tiny mouse makes the barn his house.

And in the barn lives, many of his friends,
There lives, many of his friends, with himself there's ten.

As many as ten live in the barn and play,
For, this tiny mouse makes his home in the hay.

And together they have lots of fun,
As we count his many friends starting with number one.

Number one swims and can catch fish when in luck,
Number one waddles in for number one is a duck.

Number two takes his bath in mud and will dig,
Number two is his friend the smelly old pig.

Number three is usually busy in the barn right now,
Number three supplies our milk for she is a cow.

Number four loves to run and gallop of course,
Number four wears a saddle for he is a horse.

Number five is still a friend though the tiny mouse will scat,
Number five is a little bit scary for she is a cat.

Number six barks and barks and sleeps like a log,
Number six likes to play too, because he is a dog.

Number seven has a beak and will pick and pick,
Number seven is his buddy the baby, yellow chick.

MARY MARTINA DOCKTER

Number eight sneaks in during the night somehow,
Number eight has large wings for he is an owl.

Number nine will eat anything so just take note,
Number nine is a prankster the silly old goat.

Number ten, why number ten is the mouse himself,
Number ten is the mouse for there is no one else.

For there lives in the country a barnyard mouse,
Where, this tiny mouse makes the barn his house.

And in the barn lives, many of his friends,
There lives, many of his friends, with himself there's ten.

2013

HAPPY BIRTHDAY MOUSE

"Today is my birthday," squeaked Teensy Weensy Mouse,
And she scampered down the stairs to the kitchen of her house.

But when she entered the room mother mouse wasn't there,
Just a note on the fridge saying grandma mouse was taking care.

So Teensy Weensy Mouse sat at the table eating breakfast all alone,
Feeling sorry for her self thinking her birthday wasn't known.

"I guess they all forgot," Teensy Weensy said to herself,
"So I'll celebrate my birthday with my friends, myself."

After breakfast Teensy Weensy asked grandma
mouse if she could go outside,
"Stay close by," said grandma mouse and she
whispered, "There's a big surprise."

But Teensy Weensy didn't hear grandma mouse say her little secret,
So off she went wondering about her
birthday and who to celebrate with.

"I'll ask Cathy Cat to help celebrate my special day,"
And Teensy Weensy Mouse went to see
if her friend was able to play.

But when Teensy Weensy Mouse knocked on Cathy Cat's door,
Cathy Cat's mom said her daughter went out to explore.

"I'll ask Danny Dog," Teensy Weensy Mouse said on her way,
But Danny Dog's mom also said he was unable to play.

MARY MARTINA DOCKTER

"This is strange," Teensy Weensy thought,
"Where could my friends be,
Maybe they're all at Donna Duck's just waiting for me?"

So Teensy Weensy went to visit Donna Duck's house,
Thinking her friends would be there waiting
for Teensy Weensy Mouse.

But just like before Donna Duck's mom said she wasn't there,
And Teensy Weensy wanted to cry thinking
now her friends didn't care.

"Today is my birthday and I'm the only one who knows,
For everyone has forgotten," so home Teensy Weensy Mouse goes.

But when Teensy Weensy opened the door
and entered her house that day,
Her family and friends jumped up and
cried "Surprise, happy birthday!"

For mother mouse and grandma mouse planned a party to surprise,
And Teensy Weensy unaware couldn't believe her eyes.

There were party decorations and birthday cake and ice cream,
And birthday gifts wrapped in pretty, pink, paper streams.

But best of all her family and friends were all gathered there,
Because her favorite gift knowing was that they really do care.

"Today is my birthday," squeaked Teensy Weensy Mouse,
And she celebrated a very happy birthday
with everyone in her house.

2012

BIG BROTHER AND
LITTLE SISTER MOUSE

Once upon a time there was a big brother mouse,
His name was Rylan mouse and he lived
with his family in their house.

Rylan mouse was the big brother to his baby sister mouse,
Who, he thought was too young for play in this mouse house.

His baby sister mouse was very, very silly,
And that is why her name was silly mouse Lily.

Silly Lily mouse lived up to her name,
She was always into her big brother's toys and even his games.

Rylan mouse could never play with his stuff,
Because silly mouse Lily played really, really rough.

So when big brother mouse Rylan tried to play with his blocks,
Silly Lily mouse would just tip them over with her knocks.

She knocked over his blocks she knocked over his cars,
She even knocked over his super heroes and
that made Rylan mouse see stars.

"Why does my baby sister mouse have to play in my room?
She doesn't know how to play when all
she does is make toys go boom."

And that is when silly mouse Lily started to cry,
For her big brother mouse Rylan would not even let her try.

MARY MARTINA DOCKTER

To learn how to share and play with his toys,
Big brother mouse Rylan took away her joy.

All, silly Lily mouse wanted was to play with her big brother,
Knocking over toys was her way to play, she didn't mean to bother.

Then big brother mouse Rylan decided to
share his toys when he played,
And silly mouse Lily played next to her big
brother and his toys just stayed.

Once upon a time there was a big brother named Rylan mouse,
Who, loved to play and share his toys with
his little sister, Lily mouse.

2012

FIRST DAY OF SCHOOL MOUSE

Once there was a father mouse, a mother
mouse and little Luke mouse,
And they lived together in their tiny mouse house.

Little Luke mouse stayed home with his mouse father and mother,
As he was very happy staying at home being with each other.

Their days were filled with hunting for cheese,
Only he just played around doing what he pleased.

But before they knew it little mouse Luke had grown up,
Little mouse Luke was now of age and no longer a pup.

So father mouse and mother mouse decided it was time,
For little Luke mouse to go to school and learn to find.

How to be good at hunting for food like cheese,
Because little mouse Luke when staying at
home just did what he pleased.

"I don't want to go to school and not be at home,
Father and mother mouse I'll be afraid and all alone."

Father mouse and mother mouse took little Luke mouse aside,
And each gave him a kiss and a hug until he no longer cried.

"School is where you will have many friends,
When you go to school your loneliness will end."

"And you will learn to be a good hunter just like your mom and dad,"
When suddenly little Luke mouse tears turned to glad.

MARY MARTINA DOCKTER

"I want to go to school to learn and have fun,"
Father and mother mouse were now crying
for they were proud of their son.

Once there was a father mouse and a mother
mouse in their tiny mouse house,
Because, it was the first day of school, for their little Luke mouse.

2012

ITSY BITSY BABY MOUSE

This sweet, little story being read in your house,
Is a sweet, little story about itsy bitsy baby, mouse.

For itsy bitsy baby mouse is in mommy's tummy growing inside,
And that is why itsy bitsy baby mouse is so tiny in size.

Because mommy and daddy mouse are patiently waiting with glee,
Why, they are waiting patiently with glee to be able to see.

Their precious itsy bitsy baby mouse when nine months are done,
And that is when mommy and daddy mouse
will hold their daughter or son.

But like magic mommy and daddy mouse and
doctor mouse will be able to see,
By an ultra-sound a daughter or a son itsy bitsy baby mouse will be.

For itsy bitsy baby mouse is in mommy's tummy growing inside,
And that is why itsy bitsy baby mouse is so tiny in size.

When soon itsy bitsy baby mouse's birthday will come,
And family and friends will be there to welcome the little one.

And a special, little mouse patiently waiting with care,
This special, little mouse is itsy bitsy baby
mouse's older brother there.

For itsy bitsy baby mouse is a sweet, baby girl,
She is a sweet, baby girl, with rosy cheeks and a tail that curls.

MARY MARTINA DOCKTER

And mommy and daddy mouse are happy with glee,
Why, they are happy with glee to be able to see.

Their precious itsy bitsy baby mouse, a little girl mouse so new,
Their precious, little, baby girl mouse they
named after you, Skylee Blu.

For this sweet, little story being read in your house,
Is a sweet, little story about itsy bitsy baby, mouse.

2013

A BROTHERS' MOUSE TALE

Once there lived a mouse who was his parents' favorite son,
He was their favorite son because he was the only one.

His name was Mason mouse and he loved
to play with his mom and dad,
They would play together every day and that
made Mason mouse very glad.

But one day his parents told him he would have a sister or brother,
"A sister or brother," he thought, "I don't
want to share my father or mother."

"Or my toys or my bike or my bedroom where I sleep,
I don't want to share any of my things
they're mine that I want to keep."

So Mason mouse decided when the new baby came to the house,
He would have a plan to still be his parents' favorite mouse.

"Babies are messy and they don't smell very good,
I'll be extra careful to make sure I do everything that I should."

He cleaned his room everyday and washed behind his ears,
Mason mouse did everything he could to put away his fears.

He didn't want to share his mother or father with someone new,
Just the thought of not being their favorite son made him feel blue.

MARY MARTINA DOCKTER

But the day came when mother mouse
gave birth to his baby brother,
And they brought him home to show Mason
mouse in a blanket all covered.

When Mason mouse saw his baby brother
he couldn't believe his eyes,
As mother mouse said, "This is baby Bennett
mouse," Mason mouse began to cry.

"My brother looks a lot like me I think he'll be my good friend,
I'm not afraid to share my mom and dad," so his jealousy did end.

"And I plan to share all my toys with baby
brother Bennett in our house."
So from that day forward he was known
as big brother Mason mouse.

Because once there lived two mice who
were their parents' favorite sons,
They were their favorite sons because there were two instead of one.

2012

THE THREE MOUSEKETEERS

This story is told from long ago,
It is a story of three mice brothers brave and bold.

The three brothers' mice were fashionable, too,
Why, they each wore feathers on their hats and decorative shoes.

And together they went on many adventurous travels,
As they each carried a sword so there were many battles.

Athos Mouse was the eldest brother of the three,
He was extremely intelligent for all would agree.

Aramis Mouse was the younger one of the two,
He faithfully fought for his beliefs he thought were true.

Porthos Mouse was last but not least a threesomes' brother,
So with one, two, three, the three mouseketeers had each other.

And together they went on many adventurous travels,
As they each carried a sword so there were many battles.

They fought side by side with their weapons held high,
For, they believed in truth and in justice they did cry.

And throughout the land one could hear their call,
"All for one and one for all."

MARY MARTINA DOCKTER

This story is told from long ago,
It is a story of three mice brothers brave and bold.

And like the three brothers' mice in this story you will be,
Brothers like The Mouseketeers, one, two and three.

2013

LIKE A FOX MOUSE

There once was a mouse with a big imagination,
That liked to pretend he was bigger than his creation.

Instead of wearing the usual mouse attire,
He would wear a costume of what he admired.

For this little mouse wore a fur coat the color red,
Why this little mouse would rather be a kit instead.

With big, pointed ears and a long, bushy tail,
He mimicked this creature even down to its wail.

Not only that, he began to rely,
He was truly becoming a mouse who was sly.

As none of his friends were able to peek,
And discover his hideout playing hide-and-seek.

When competing with classmates on the long jump,
No one came close to his jumping rump.

Even his mom and dad had to admit,
Their little mouse was sneakier a little bit.

For when it was time to go to bed,
He had his parents reading a book to him instead.

Because once there was a mouse with a big imagination,
That liked to pretend he was bigger than his creation.

MARY MARTINA DOCKTER

Instead of wearing the usual mouse attire,
He would wear a costume of what he admired.

And that is why he was then called in his house,
Like a fox, this little mouse.

2015

THE LITTLE PRINCESS MOUSE

Once upon a time in a faraway land,
There lived a little mouse, Emmy, with a story so grand.

She imagined herself a princess to be,
But a sister to boss to her brothers' three.

And this little mouse's beauty was so fair,
The fairest of all the other mice compared.

Lived in the forest faraway,
Far, from the castle where her dreams stayed.

Within a fantasy, there a prince would be,
This prince in armor she would see.

In her dream he'd gather flowers in the darkest of night,
So no one would see that he was a knight.

That gave her the bouquet to win her heart,
As he would take her hand to then depart.

And together they'd enter the castle on the hill,
But soon she would awake and in the forest still.

With a vision so real she could feel his hand,
Hold her hand on the way to his kingdom's land.

But she dare not say a word to her brothers three,
That guarded her like a prisoner who might flee.

For they didn't want the burden of dishes to do,
When, they had a sister to boss with no clue.

Why just because they're older did not mean,
She was to do all their work and clean.

Then one night when she was falling asleep,
A magical star awoke her from the deep.

And by her bed flowers did appear,
For, it was not a dream but the prince was near.

And together they entered the castle on the hill,
As she was awake and no longer in the forest still.

But her brothers three left to do the chores in the house,
Their sister, Emmy, is now the little princess mouse.

2017

TWIN SISTERS, MICE

Once there were sisters, mice that were twins,
And this is how their story begins.

The sisters, mice, were the best of friends,
They were the best of friends in this story when.

They did everything together which was nice,
Because Chrissie mouse and Teensy mouse were twin mice.

And together they would play and play,
They would play together every day.

For Chrissie mouse and Teensy mouse played very special games,
As one special game was being a mirror for they looked the same.

And whatever one did so did the other,
With their noses scrunching and whiskers
bunching they looked like each other.

They were always able to play hide-and-seek,
As one would hide, one would peek.

And they enjoyed a good game of cat and mouse,
When, chasing each other around the house.

Why they even played a special game of jump rope,
By tying their long tails together they took turns jumping in hope.

Together they would play and play,
They would play together every day.

                                        MARY MARTINA DOCKTER

Because Chrissie mouse and Teensy mouse were twin mice,
And they did everything together which was nice.

The sisters, mice, were the best of friends,
They were the best of friends in this story when.

Once there were sisters, mice that were twins,
And this is how their story ends.

2013

BEST OF FRIENDS MICE

Two little mice were the best of friends,
And this is how their story begins.

For the two little mice lived in two little houses,
And they lived next door to each other the two little mouses.

The one little mouse wore nothing but red,
Red was her favorite color, wearing a red bow on her head.

The other little mouse, mouse number two,
Wore a different color dress for her favorite color was blue.

And in the beginning they would not play with each other,
Not with one mouse wearing red, and wearing blue, the other.

Because mouse number one would never, ever wave hi,
When, mouse number two who wore blue came by.

And mouse number two never, ever said,
Why anything nice to mouse number one because she wore red.

So that is where this story will begin,
With mouse number one and mouse
number two not speaking when.

Their mouse mothers decided something had to be done,
For mouse number one and mouse number
two did not care to have fun.

When, playing alone without a good friend,
Their mouse mothers knew this had to end.

MARY MARTINA DOCKTER

So mouse number one's mother bought her a dress that was blue,
And mouse number one really liked it, who knew.

Then mouse number two's mother bought her a dress that was red,
And mouse number two really liked it, she said.

And that is when they began to play with each other,
When, mouse number one and mouse
number two switched their colors.

And became the best of friends the two little mice,
So they played together and were very nice.

For two little mice lived in two little houses,
And they lived next door to each other the two little mouses.

The two little mice were the best of friends,
They were the best of friends is how their story ends.

2013

THIS IS BIG THIS IS LITTLE MOUSE

Once there was an inquisitive mouse who, always compared,
Everything he would see in sight for his curious eye was there.

And there he would stare at everything he would see,
From the largest object to the smallest one to be.

For the curious mouse would look at a tree and say, "This is big,"
And then be under the tree to say,
"This is little," at a bug he would dig.

"The tree is big, the bug is little," he would say,
"The tree is big, the bug is little," he would say as he played.

For then the curious mouse would look at
a house and say, "This is big,"
And then see his sister and say, "This is little," as she was doing a jig.

"The house is big, the mouse is little," he would say,
"The house is big, the mouse is little," he would say as he played.

And then the curious mouse would look up at the sky and say,
"This is big." And then look at himself and
say, "This is little," as he did.

"The sky is big, I am little," he would say,
"The sky is big, I am little," he would say as he played.

MARY MARTINA DOCKTER

Because there he would stare at everything he would see,
From the largest object to the smallest one to be.

For once there was an inquisitive mouse who, always compared,
Everything he would see in sight for his curious eye was there.

2013

MAJESTIC MICE

There lives a family of mice in the South Dakota hills,
Where, this family of mice, live within, its monuments still.

And in this family of mice are two mice brothers,
One with the name of Charlie mouse and Lakota mouse the other.

Charlie mouse is very proud of his name,
For, he was named after Mr. Charles Rushmore which is the same.

And that is why Charlie mouse takes pride in what he does,
When, Charlie mouse watches over Mt. Rushmore because.

Mt. Rushmore is a majestic monument
depicting the faces of U.S. Presidents,
George Washington, Thomas Jefferson, Abraham
Lincoln, and Theodore Roosevelt take residence.

So Charlie mouse has a big job even though he is very small,
With the enormous carved heads reaching a
height of 60 feet so they are very tall.

But Charlie mouse doesn't mind for he is always there you see,
When, he watches over Mt. Rushmore known
as the "Shrine of Democracy".

There lives a family of mice in the South Dakota hills,
Where, this family of mice, live within, its monuments still.

And in this family of mice are two mice brothers,
One with the name of Charlie mouse and Lakota mouse the other.

Lakota mouse is very proud of his name,
For, he was named after the Sioux Indians of
this mountain which is the same.

And that is why Lakota mouse takes pride in what he does,
When, Lakota mouse watches over the stone
sculpture of Crazy Horse because.

Crazy Horse is a majestic monument honoring
the Native American Indian,
Located not far from Mt. Rushmore, it is devoted
to preserve Indian culture and tradition.

So Lakota mouse has a big job even though he is very small,
With the spirit of Crazy Horse, his humility
and valor which is very tall.

But Lakota mouse doesn't mind for he is always there you see,
When he watches over the sculpture of Crazy
Horse a heritage of its people he believes.

There lives a family of mice in the South Dakota hills,
Where, this family of mice, live within, its monuments still.

And in this family of mice are two mice brothers,
One with the name of Charlie mouse and Lakota mouse the other.

For Charlie mouse and Lakota mouse watch
over majestic monuments twice,
As the monument of Mt. Rushmore and Crazy
Horse are honored by majestic mice.

2013

THE MASSIVE MAMMOTH MOUSE

There is a little mouse who lives in a grand museum,
For in this museum is where people come to see them.

The many amazing exhibits at the museum of natural history,
As that is where fossils are displayed at the archive of mystery.

But there is one special exhibit people come to see,
It is the exhibit with this little mouse for it is hard to believe.

This little mouse who, shares his house with bones of old,
Loves to explore the floor where dinosaurs roam it is told.

For this little mouse is happy to be because he is so very small,
When, he is with the dinosaurs because they are so very tall.

He runs around until it is found his favorite one of all,
The woolly, massive mammoth he believes is the grandest one of all.

With a hump on its back, woolly, long hair
and tusks just like an elephant,
This little mouse did make a best friend for it is quite elegant.

Because the woolly, massive mammoth just like
the little mouse burrow in the earth,
As the woolly, massive mammoth eats plants
just like the little mouse since birth.

For this little mouse is happy to be because he is so very small,
When, he is with his best friend the woolly, massive
mammoth because he is so very tall.

MARY MARTINA DOCKTER

And together they share their house with bones of old,
This little mouse and the woolly, massive mammoth
where other dinosaurs roam it's told.

With all the exhibits at the museum of natural history,
As that is where fossils are displayed at the archive of mystery.

But there is one special exhibit people come to see,
It is the exhibit with this little mouse for it is hard to believe.

There is a little mouse who, lives in a grand museum,
Where, this little mouse sits on top a woolly,
massive mammoth so people can see them.

2013

MOTHER NATURE MOUSE

There lives in the forest at the edge of a knoll,
A simple, little rodent, whose home, is a hole.

And this simple, little rodent with his whiskers is a mouse,
Why with his whiskers he is able to clean up his tiny house.

For this simple, little rodent takes good care of his home,
When, he sweeps with his whiskers, his home near a dome.

And with his sharp teeth he is able to pick up any litter nearby,
His home is his castle and that is the reason why.

This simple, little rodent takes good care of his home,
When, in the forest this simple, little mouse is not alone.

All the animals living in the forest take good care,
They take good care of the forest for that is where.

Mother Nature is there and keeps them warm,
She feeds them when they're hungry and protects them from harm.

Mother Nature takes care of each animal in the wild,
All the animals in the forest for each animal, is her child.

And that is why this simple, little rodent
takes good care of his house,
For Mother Nature provides such a good
home for this simple, little mouse.

　　　　　　　　　　　MARY MARTINA DOCKTER

And this simple, little rodent with his whiskers will sweep,
Why with his whiskers he is able to keep his home neat.

For, there lives in the forest at the edge of a knoll,
A simple, little mouse, whose home, is a hole.

2013

THE MOUSE IN
THE ZOOKEEPER'S POCKET

In the middle of a small town there is a small, little zoo,
And in this small, little zoo there is a zookeeper, too.

The zookeeper takes care of all the animals there,
And in the zookeeper's pocket there is a mouse who also shares.

With helping the zookeeper feed the animals in the zoo,
For in the zookeeper's pocket the mouse can get around, too.

And together the zookeeper with the mouse
in his pocket have, a busy day,
For early in the morning the barn animals
at the petting zoo need their hay.

So the mouse in the zookeeper's pocket knows just what to do,
When cleaning out the barn by replacing the old hay with new.

And the pony, the goat and all the barn animals are happy to see,
Why the zookeeper and the mouse in his pocket with glee.

Now the zookeeper with the mouse in his
pocket feed the tiger and the lion,
As, they need to be extra careful not to disturb
their sleep where they lie in.

When the zookeeper with the mouse in his
pocket feed the silly, silly monkey,
The monkey has the zookeeper and the mouse
in his pocket laughing, he is so funny.

MARY MARTINA DOCKTER

And not to forget all the exotic birds in their cages as they sing,
When, the zookeeper with the mouse in his
pocket have special bird food they bring.

Last but not least the zookeeper with the mouse
in his pocket feed the tortoise in his shell,
And the tortoise in his shell and the other animals
are thankful for they are doing so well.

Because in the middle of a small town there is a small, little zoo,
And in this small, little zoo there is a zookeeper, too.

So by the end of the day all the animals are
fed before the zookeeper locks it,
And, says goodnight to the zoo with a very
special friend the mouse in his pocket.

2013

BE UNIQUE MOUSE

A little mouse gazed in the mirror in his house,
And said, "This is me in the mirror," smiled the little mouse.

"I am me and no other mouse is just like me,"
The little mouse looked in the mirror once again to see.

He wiggled his nose and blinked his eyes,
Why, the little mouse even gave his long whiskers a try.

It was then the little mouse jumped off a tiny chair where he sat,
Being pleased with himself and that was that.

But it didn't take long before he met another mouse,
And it was like looking in the mirror at himself in his house.

So the little mouse spied again at the other mouse to see,
Was he looking at another mouse or in a mirror of, he.

Because they both wiggled their noses and blinked their eyes,
Why, the little mice even gave their long whiskers a try.

For then the little mouse soon realized there
were other mice just like him,
Who could wiggle their noses and blink their
eyes with whiskers above their chins.

"But I am me and no other mouse is just like me," he cried,
And off he scampered but not as merrily as before he realized.

The little mouse was so puzzled all he could
do was run as fast as he could,
Why, he ran even faster than any other mouse would.

                              MARY MARTINA DOCKTER

And then the little mouse knew there were
no other mice just like him,
Who could run as fast in a race and be the one to win.

Because when the little mouse gazed at
himself in the mirror in his house,
He would say, "This is me, be unique," smiled the little mouse.

2013

BE DIFFERENT MOUSE

Here in the forest lives many a mouse,
Where, each little mouse has the same type of house.

The same type of house burrowed into the ground,
Where, each little mouse lives in dark all around.

So a mouse is unable to see the rise of the sun,
When living in a dark hole just like everyone.

But here in the forest is a mouse not the same,
Where, this little mouse lives puts the other mice to shame.

Instead of living in a hole burrowed into the dark ground,
This little mouse lives up in a tree and can see all around.

He wakes up in the morning to watch the rise of the sun,
And he is in bed to watch the sunset when the day is done.

But here in the forest the other mice do not understand why,
Why this little mouse lives up in the tree so close to the sky.

When living underground is what many a mouse, do,
Why the other mice in the forest they have not a clue.

Because here in the forest is a mouse not the same,
He lives up in a tree and that is his fame.

When here in the forest lives many a mouse,
Where, each little mouse has the same type of house.

But here in the forest is a mouse with his own type of house,
Where, he dares to be different among many a mouse.

2013

NEVER GIVE UP MOUSE

In an enchanted forest there lived a little mouse,
Where, this little mouse and his mice
family lived in their mouse house.

And in this mice family there were many sisters and brothers,
But this little mouse was the tiniest so he was just a bother.

When all he wanted was their help to learn how to do new things,
Like how to jump up high but they wouldn't show him a thing.

Because they would say, "You're too tiny," then scurry away,
As this little mouse felt even tinier than he was anyway.

So this little mouse decided he would find someone new to ask,
On how to jump up high for he struggled doing the task.

But on the way he came across a little bird on the ground,
For this little bird was flapping its wings making a funny sound.

"What are you trying to do?" Squeaked the little mouse,
"Why I'm trying to fly, fly, fly," chirped
the little bird, "fly to my house."

"But don't you need someone's help," the little mouse asked,
"Not if I keep trying and never give up," said
the little bird, "I can do this task."

And sure enough the little bird started to fly, fly, fly away,
So this little mouse decided he would find
someone new to ask that day.

MARY MARTINA DOCKTER

But on the way he came across a little squirrel on the ground,
For this little squirrel was running around making a funny sound.

"What are you trying to do?" Squeaked the little mouse,
"Why I'm trying to climb high, high, high," said
the little squirrel, "climb to my house."

"But don't you need someone's help," the little mouse asked,
"Not if I keep trying and never give up," said
the little squirrel, "I can do this task."

And sure enough the little squirrel started to
climb high, high, high up in the tree,
And it is then this little mouse began to really, really see.

What it means to really try, try, try, and not to rest,
When never giving up on a task by doing your very best.

So this little mouse decided he would
learn to jump high on his own,
And not only did he learn to jump high but he had also grown.

In an enchanted forest there lived a little mouse,
Where, this little mouse always keeps trying
and never gives up in his house.

2013

MESSY, MESSY MOUSE

This is a story about a messy, messy mouse,
Who never cleaned his room in his mouse, house.

Messy, messy mouse leaves his toys everywhere,
He leaves his toys everywhere as if he doesn't care.

And that is why his toys feel very sad and blue,
When, they're not taken care of even when they're new.

Because messy, messy mouse leaves his toys everywhere,
His toys decided to find a new home that really cared.

One day when messy, messy mouse went into his room to play,
All of his toys were gone because they had gone away.

His blocks, his cars and even his favorite choo choo train gone,
Why all of his toys were not in his room where they belong.

"Where are all my toys?" Messy, messy mouse did cry,
"They were all in my room where I had left them lie."

And that is when mother mouse took messy, messy mouse aside,
Telling him his toys were very sad because he doesn't even try.

To clean his room and keep his toys safe from any harm,
And that is why mother mouse squeaked the alarm.

Because messy, messy mouse leaves his toys everywhere,
When his toys only wanted to know that he really cared.

                    MARY MARTINA DOCKTER

So messy, messy mouse began to clean his room before he played,
And all of his toys, they all came back that very same day.

This is a story about not a messy, messy mouse,
Who always cleaned his room in his mouse, house.

2013

PLEASE AND THANK YOU MOUSE

There once was a little mouse with manners no good,
For this little mouse did not do what a little mouse should.

Instead of asking nicely for something that he saw,
This little mouse went into a tantrum with screaming and all.

He would lie on the floor kicking and
crying and there he would stay,
Oh, this little mouse made quite a scene until he got his own way.

Until one day he realized he wasn't getting anywhere,
His kicking and crying did nothing more
than make other mice stare.

"There must be another way to let my parents know," he thought,
"There must be another way of asking," so this little mouse sought.

To find the secret he was missing in all that he would ask,
Why this little mouse believed there must be a secret task.

But this little mouse soon discovered the secret was out,
By saying please and thank you there was no need to pout.

So this little mouse began to say please
and thank you during the day,
And this little mouse instead of kicking and
crying had more time then to play.

There once was a little mouse with manners so good,
For he would say please and thank you and do what he should.

2012

                    MARY MARTINA DOCKTER

HOW TO BE HAPPY MOUSE

There lived a mouse very rich,
But he wanted more and more to enrich.

He was never satisfied with what he had,
The thought of wanting more made him sad.

Even though his plate was always full,
It wasn't enough for him to drool.

And this very rich mouse had no clue,
How to be happy, the golden rule.

There lived a mouse that was poor,
But he never took for granted wanting more.

He was thankful and grateful for what he had,
The thought of his blessings made him glad.

Even though his plate was sometimes a shame,
It wasn't enough for him to complain.

For this mouse that was poor had a clue,
How to be happy, the golden rule.

2017

THE BRAVE LITTLE MOUSE

In a far away land many years ago,
There lived a mouse and a man both with the
name of Daniel the story is told.

Daniel mouse was known throughout the Mice
Kingdom as a very honest mouse,
As was the man named Daniel for he was
trustworthy just like Daniel mouse.

For the story is told both mouse and man
worked hard and in God they obeyed,
When in Babylon of ancient Middle East to
obey God was forbidden in those days.

So many a mouse were jealous of Daniel mouse
with his success rising to the top,
And also the man named Daniel with his success
in the government thus wouldn't stop.

Then mice and men decided to use faith in God
against this man and Daniel mouse,
As they, tricked King Darius into passing a decree
against praying to God in any house.

But Daniel mouse and the man named Daniel
did not worry about this strife,
Just as they have always done, they went home,
knelt down and thanked God for life.

                    MARY MARTINA DOCKTER

The wicked mice and men caught Daniel mouse
and the man when praying to God,
As King Darius who loved both Daniels
could only give the order with a nod.

When at sundown they threw Daniel mouse
and Daniel the man into the lions den,
For King Darius could not eat or sleep all through the night when.

At dawn the King ran to the lions cage and asked
if God protected them, Daniel replied,
"My God sent his angel and he shut the mouths
of the lions," he cried. (Daniel 6:22)

And scripture says, "The King was overjoyed
and Daniel was brought out unharmed,"
(Daniel 6:23) When, their trust in God
kept them safe in his loving arms.

For in a far away land many years ago,
Their lived a mouse and a man both with the
name of Daniel, the story is told.

And Daniel mouse was known within the Mice
Kingdom as a very brave, little mouse,
As, was the man named Daniel who was very
courageous just like Daniel mouse.

2013

THE MIGHTY LITTLE MOUSE

This story begins many years ago,
About a little mouse and a young man many seem to know.

I'm sure you've heard the story of David and Goliath,
But did you know there was a little mouse who had also triumphed.

It was when the Philistine Army gathered
against the Army of Israel for war,
A giant named Goliath for forty days mocked
and challenged them to the core.

And there on the battlefield was also an army of mice,
Who, gathered together against the army
of rats that weren't very nice.

For within the army of rats was a giant of a
rat, challenging the mice to fight,
His name was Goliath the Rat and he mocked
the mice both day and night.

And as the story goes a young man named David
volunteered to fight for King Saul,
When, a mouse named David also volunteered
even though he was very small.

Then both mouse and young man with only a
sling shot and a pouch filled with stones,
Why, they approached the giants that cursed
at them but they were not alone.

MARY MARTINA DOCKTER

The young man David said to the Philistine,
"You come against me with sword and spear and javelin,
but I come against you in the name of the Lord,"
1 Samuel 17
For the mouse named David and the young
man then threw their stones towards.

Hitting Goliath the Rat and Goliath the
Philistine with one sling shot to the head,
As both giants fell to the ground, they were now dead.

And the army of rats and the Philistine Army turned and ran away,
Because a little mouse and a young man were very brave that day.

As the story ends many years ago, this young man
becomes King David of God's house,
And this little mouse named David was known
by all as the mighty, little mouse.

2013

THE LOYAL LITTLE MOUSE

Long ago when this story was new,
There was a little mouse named Ruth and
a young woman named Ruth, too.

And together they lived in Naomi's house,
Her daughter in-law named Ruth and this little mouse.

But Naomi tells them they should leave,
When, they are not of her faith and do not believe.

But the young woman Ruth and this little mouse,
They are faithful to this Israelite in her house.

For Ruth tells Naomi, "Where you go I will
go and where you stay I will stay,"
Ruth 1: 16 & 17
As, the little mouse Ruth and this young woman pray.

And together they return to the town of Bethlehem,
Where this little mouse and young woman Ruth obeys God's plan.

To harvest barley as they work in the fields,
It is there they support Naomi and themselves by its yield.

For the Book of Ruth tells of this history,
As, a little mouse named Ruth remains a mystery.

Because long ago when this story was new,
There was a little mouse named Ruth and
a young woman named Ruth, too.

And together they lived in Naomi's house,
With this young woman who was loyal, and the loyal, little mouse.

2013

STORYBOOK MOUSE

There once was a little, little mouse that lived under a nook,
And under the nook this little, little mouse would read his book.

He would read his book throughout the day,
As he would rather read than go out and play.

For this little, little mouse had the biggest imagination,
And that is why this little, little mouse read with determination.

Because whenever this little, little mouse
read his book under the nook,
He was able to imagine himself, himself in the book.

Why this little, little mouse imagined
himself a pirate on a daring trip,
And on many adventures he looked for treasure with his pirate ship.

This little, little mouse was once a brave knight heading towards,
There to slay the dragon and rescue the princess with his sword.

This little, little mouse was even once a horse that raced,
And it was pretty funny imagining himself with a horse's face.

Why this little, little mouse even imagined going to the moon,
As he orbits the moon with his spaceship before he lands soon.

For this little, little mouse had the biggest imagination,
And that is why this little, little mouse read with determination.

MARY MARTINA DOCKTER

Because he would whittle away the pages while reading his book,
Whenever, this little, little mouse would
read his book under the nook.

There under the nook this little, little
mouse would read in his house,
And that is why this little, little mouse was the storybook mouse.

2013

CINDERELLA MOUSE

Once upon a time in an enchanted, far away land,
There lived a little girl mouse with a story so grand.

This little girl mouse lived with her dear, devoted father,
For it was just the two of them since the death of her mother.

But this little girl mouse knew she was dearly loved,
Not only, from her caring, devoted father
but from her mother above.

And her life was full and complete she had truly thought,
As her kind, devoted father surprised her
with the many gifts he had bought.

Then one day her father married again a
mouse from a good family of mice,
And his new mouse wife had daughters
about little girl mouse age by twice.

So now she thought everything would be perfectly fine,
She had a new stepmother mouse and
two new stepsister mice divine.

But it wasn't until the untimely death of her father,
her stepmother's true nature showed,
How jealous she was of little girl mouse's beauty
her two mice daughters did not know.

And eventually poor little girl mouse became
a servant in her own house,
Thus she was always cooking and cleaning, so
they named her Cinderella mouse.

But Cinderella mouse was still very cheerful
and always happy you see,
Because in her heart she knew her dream
of true love would come to be.

And there from her tiny bedroom window the
royal mouse palace was in full sight,
As Cinderella mouse would make a wish each and every night.

For Cinderella mouse would keep her wish
to herself because she knew,
A dream must be kept to oneself for a dream to come true.

When over at the royal mouse palace the
mouse King was extremely upset,
For the mouse Prince was to return home
without his mouse bride still yet.

So the mouse King ordered the mouse Duke
to plan a royal ball for that very night,
As every mouse maiden would be invited so the
Prince will have them all in his sight.

And the mouse King chuckled to himself
thinking his son will be able to pick,
A mouse bride for himself not knowing he had been tricked.

So while Cinderella mouse was cleaning she
heard a loud knock at the front door,
It was a message from the mouse King to announce
the Prince is home from his explore.

For Cinderella mouse knew the letter would be
important so she quickly took it upstairs,
To where her stepmother mouse and stepsister
mice were singing and surely unaware.

Then stepmother mouse became very upset for
Cinderella mouse disturbed their song,
While the ugly stepsister mice are trying to
sing Cinderella mouse does not belong.

"But stepmother mouse," Cinderella cried, "an
urgent message arrived from the King,"
The two ugly stepsisters snatched the letter
from Cinderella before she could bring.

When stepmother mouse grabbed the letter from
her daughters she started to read aloud,
"There shall be a royal ball in honor of the Prince
with every eligible maiden around."

"And we're so eligible," cried the two ugly
stepsister mice as they began to dance,
When Cinderella mouse said, "why, that includes
me," hoping she might have a chance.

"Yes," squeaked stepmother mouse, "IF, you
are able to get all your work done,"
As the stepsister mice began to complain, she
said again "IF," knowing she had won.

But Cinderella mouse was very excited and went
to her room to check out her dress,
Thinking it was a little old fashioned, she could
fix that, but they gave her no rest.

"Cinderella mouse won't go to the ball," her
tiny, insect friends all began to say,
"They'll fix it so she won't be able to go, by
making her do extra work today."

                    MARY MARTINA DOCKTER

"We can do it!" cheered the crickets as they
began to sing their merry song,
And together they helped Cinderella mouse fix
her dress so she too could go along.

Now at the end of the day Cinderella mouse
told them the carriage had arrived,
"You're not ready?" squeaked stepmother
mouse knowing she had lied.

"Well, there will be other times," stepmother
mouse said making it seem alright,
And they rushed to get out of the house
before saying their goodnight.

Cinderella mouse silently went into her room
and stared out of her window when,
"Surprise, surprise!" cried the tiny crickets as
her new dress was displayed then.

"Why it's beautiful!" Cinderella mouse
squeaked not believing her eyes,
"Wait for me." she said as she ran down the
stairs. "Do you like it?" was her reply.

"Mother mouse it's not fair." the stepsister
mice cried making a horrible sound,
"Daughters do you like her sash and these beads?"
When, she knew they were found.

"Why you little thief!" they said ripping Cinderella's dress apart,
Stepmother mouse had a sinister grin leaving
her dress tattered while they depart.

Poor Cinderella mouse ran out of the house
into the garden where she cried,
"It's hopeless," she said over and over believing all hope had died.

But Cinderella mouse was unaware her one
wish was about to come true,
When, her godmother mouse magically and
suddenly came from out of the blue.

"Hopeless, why if it was hopeless how could
I be here with you tonight,"
Then godmother mouse dried Cinderella's
tears, waving her wand in sight.

And before Cinderella's eyes, a beautiful
carriage appeared ready for her to ride,
With Cinderella mouse wearing a stunning
gown, and glass slippers," she cried.

But godmother mouse wamed Cinderella mouse
her wish was only until midnight,
For when the spell is broken all will go back to
the way it was before this very night.

Cinderella entered the palace when the Prince
was with other mouse maidens there,
And as Cinderella mouse entered the palace
the mouse Prince and everyone stared.

The mouse Prince took Cinderella's hand
and together they started to dance,
The mouse King had ordered a waltz hoping
true love might have a chance.

     MARY MARTINA DOCKTER

And as they danced the other mouse maidens
looked on wondering who she was,
Why even stepmother mouse and her ugly
stepsisters asked who she was because.

Stepmother mouse thought for a moment and
recognized her, but was unable to see,
When the mouse Duke gave them privacy
she was not able to see to believe.

So Cinderella mouse and the mouse Prince
danced throughout the night,
Then suddenly the clock gave the alarm for
it was now the strike of midnight.

And Cinderella mouse cried, "I must go
because at midnight I must leave,"
"But I do not know your name," sighed the
Prince for he could hardly believe.

Cinderella mouse ran out of the palace with
only her glass slipper to remind,
The mouse Prince of Cinderella's beauty for he
swore to the mouse king he would find.

By having every mouse maiden in the kingdom
try on the glass slipper, he said,
So the mouse Duke was ordered to find the
maiden before he could go to bed.

Stepmother mouse called for Cinderella mouse
to get ready her stepsister mice,
For the mouse Duke would soon be arriving and
stepmother wanted them to look nice.

"What for?" the stepsister mice cried wanting to go back to bed,
"Why the Prince is looking for the maiden who
lost her slipper." stepmother mouse said.

"But what does that have to do with us?" They
sighed pulling the covers over their heads,
"Listen to me, no one knows who she is so
both of you have a chance." she said.

"We do!" they cried and ordered Cinderella
mouse to get them ready in time,
"What's wrong with her?" They thought
Cinderella mouse was out of her mind.

For Cinderella mouse dropped the breakfast tray
and started to dance and sing a song,
As stepmother mouse eyes squinted she could
see it was Cinderella mouse all along.

So stepmother followed Cinderella mouse up
the stairs to lock her in her room,
She did not want Cinderella mouse try on the
glass slipper for it would mean her doom.

Because stepmother mouse wanted one of her
daughters to marry the mouse Prince,
And with Cinderella mouse out of the way they
would have a chance to marry since.

Cinderella mouse was locked in her room she
begged for stepmother mouse to let her go,
But stepmother mouse gave an eerie squeak as
she turned away for she did not know.

                    MARY MARTINA DOCKTER

The tiny crickets wanted to help and told
Cinderella mouse they would get the key,
And quietly they climbed up to stepmother's
pocket and secretly the key was retrieved.

So while the mouse Duke was trying the glass
slipper on the ugly stepsister mice feet,
The tiny crickets unlocked Cinderella's bolted
door so stepmother mouse would be beat.

And as the mouse Duke asked if there were any
other maidens to try on the slipper then,
Cinderella mouse ran down the stairs begging,
"Can I try on the glass slipper?" When.

Stepmother mouse and the ugly stepsister mice
tried to keep the mouse Duke away,
"She is just an imaginative child, why it is
just Cinderella mouse." they did say.

"Every eligible maiden." answered the mouse
Duke taking Cinderella's petite paw,
But as the glass slipper was being brought to
him, stepmother mouse tripped the law.

For the glass slipper flew up in the air and
it shattered when it hit the floor,
The mouse Duke put his paws to his face for
the King would be mad to the core.

"Oh what will he say, Oh what will he do!" The
mouse Duke cried for it was done,
As stepmother mouse and her ugly daughters
smiled knowing they had won.

"But will this help, I have the other glass slipper?"
Cinderella mouse held out her shoe,
For the mouse Duke placed the glass slipper
on Cinderella so then everyone knew.

"It fits, it fits!" Mouse Duke proclaimed with
stepmother and her daughters looking on,
For Cinderella mouse would no longer be their
house servant but a Princess from now on.

And within the kingdom the King invited all to
the wedding of Cinderella and the Prince,
But not Cinderella's stepmother nor her ugly
daughters for they haven't been seen since.

For once upon a time in an enchanted, far away land,
Cinderella mouse and the mouse Prince lived
happily ever after, a story so grand.

2013

                              MARY MARTINA DOCKTER

THE TOOTH FAIRY MOUSE

Under the pillow is where one puts their tooth,
When, one loses their tooth but do you know the truth.

How the tooth fairy gets under the pillow in your house,
Why, the tooth fairy has a special worker that is a mouse.

And the tooth fairy keeps the mouse in her pocket,
As she flies from house to house, this little mouse may unlock it.

The mystery of how she is able to take,
All the children's teeth under their pillows without them awake.

When the tooth fairy flutters close to one's head,
She opens her pocket and out comes the little mouse on the bed.

And the little mouse knows just what to do,
She wiggles her nose because she knows the secret, too.

How the tooth fairy gets under the pillow in your house,
Why, the tooth fairy has a special worker that is a mouse.

And the little mouse as quiet as a mouse slowly crawls underneath,
As she uses her tail to then retrieve your teeth.

But before she takes the tooth that is there,
She makes sure she leaves a gift of money with care.

For under the pillow is where one puts their tooth,
When, one loses their tooth but do you know the truth.

How the tooth fairy gets under the pillow in your house,
Why, the tooth fairy has a special worker the tooth fairy mouse.

2013

MARY MARTINA DOCKTER

TICK TOCK MOUSE

Once there was a mouse, who never kept time,
This little mouse was always late and always in a bind.

And because this little mouse did not keep a clock,
He never knew the time was by its tick tock.

So he didn't seem to mind always being late,
As he came and went on his own time, thinking it was great.

For this little mouse was late to school long after the bell rings,
And he was always late for choir practice long after everyone sings.

Because this little mouse just came and went on his own time,
As he didn't seem to mind thinking everything was fine.

But soon the day came when at school there was a big test,
Oh this little mouse missed it since he was home still at rest.

And that same day the choir sang in the school play,
But this little mouse missed it when he was late again that day.

Then this little mouse began to think maybe he should keep time,
And then this little mouse would not be late and always in a bind.

So now he goes to school long before the bell rings,
And this little mouse is at choir practice long before everyone sings.

For once there was a mouse, who always kept time,
As this little mouse was never late and never in a bind.

Because this little mouse got himself his own little clock,
And now he is always, always on time by its tick tock.

2013

MARY MARTINA DOCKTER

NIGHTY-NIGHT MOUSE

Once upon a time not so long ago,
There lived a tiny, little mouse and to bed he wouldn't go.

For when it was time for bed as night time came around,
This tiny, little mouse was no where to be found.

Because when it was time for him to go to bed,
This tiny, little mouse had visions in his head.

"I don't want to go to bed and sleep in my room,"
For this tiny, little mouse was afraid, it was assumed.

"There's nothing to be frightened of," his
mother and father had said,
So together with tiny, little mouse they brought him back to bed.

"My room is too dark when the day turns into night."
So mother mouse put in his room his own night light.

"There's something in my closet when you shut my door,"
So father mouse took tiny, little mouse there to explore.

And together they discovered nothing was ever there,
But tiny, little mouse did have quite a scare.

"What about under my bed, I know something touches my arm,"
So father mouse looked under his bed to
make sure nothing does him harm.

Then tiny, little mouse decided to look under his bed,
too. And together they discovered nothing
was ever there to say BOO!

So mother and father mouse had tiny, little mouse brush his teeth,
For, tiny, little mouse was getting ready for
bed since nothing was underneath.

They covered him with a blanket in his tiny, little bed,
And then he listened to a story as his favorite book was read.

They brought him his treasured toy, his cuddly teddy bear,
And kissed him on his cheek to show they really care.

When all was quiet and calm in the mouse house,
Mother and father whispered, "nighty-
night" to their tiny, little mouse.

For once upon a time not so long ago,
There lived a tiny, little mouse and to bed he would go.

2013

                                    MARY MARTINA DOCKTER

WHEN I GROW UP MOUSE

In a very small house lives a tiny, little mouse,
But this tiny, little mouse has a big
imagination for such a small mouse.

Because this tiny, little mouse thinks about
what he wants to be when he grows up,
When this tiny, little mouse dreams, he is no longer a pup.

For this tiny, little mouse is still very, very young,
As he has much older brothers and sisters his life has just begun.

But every night before he falls asleep in his bed,
This tiny, little mouse thinks about his future ahead.

He lies in bed when lights are out, all alone,
And that is when this tiny, little mouse dreams he is grown.

Oh, this tiny, little mouse imagines himself a firefighter mouse,
As he rides in a big, red fire mouse truck to
put a fire out at a mouse house.

This tiny, little mouse imagines himself a police officer mouse,
As sirens scream on his police mouse car as
he tries to catch the bad, bad mouse.

This tiny, little mouse imagines himself a racecar driver mouse,
When, he races around the track with the
other mice to be the winner mouse.

This tiny, little mouse imagines himself a zookeeper mouse,
When, he takes care of lions, tigers and
elephants in the mouse zoo house.

This tiny, little mouse imagines himself a
dinosaur, paleontologist mouse,
When, he digs up pre-historic dinosaur mice
bones to put in the mouse museum house.

This tiny, little mouse imagines himself a doctor mouse,
And he helps to cure sick mice while
working in a mouse hospital house.

Why this tiny, little mouse even imagines himself a daddy mouse,
And he has a big mouse family just like
his family in their mouse house.

But this tiny, little mouse is still very, very young.
As he has much older brothers and sisters his life has just begun.

But every night before he falls asleep in his bed,
This tiny, little mouse thinks about his future ahead.

Because this tiny, little mouse thinks about
what he wants to be when he grows up,
When this tiny, little mouse dreams he is no longer a pup.

For in a very small house lives a tiny, little mouse,
But this tiny, little mouse has the biggest
imagination for such a small mouse.

2013

                                    MARY MARTINA DOCKTER

THE LITTLE NURSE MOUSE

There is a little mouse, who resides in a hospital as her house,
And in her house she takes care of all the sick mice this little mouse.

In a room where there are other patients sleeping in their beds,
There is a tiny hole in the wall where mice
patients are sleeping instead.

And there the mice patients have runny noses,
a bad cough and a fever from the flu,
But this little mouse in her white uniform knows just what to do.

For this little mouse has a tiny, tiny thermometer in her paw,
When she takes their temperature and
gives out medicine to them all.

She keeps them safe and warm with blankets she has there,
As she stays by their bedside until they feel
better because she really cares.

So after she makes her rounds she scribbles
in their medical mouse charts,
Why this little mouse is a guardian angel with such a helpful heart.

For where there are other patients sleeping in their beds,
There is a tiny hole in the wall where mice
patients are sleeping instead.

And there the mice patients are much better from the flu,
Because a little mouse in her white uniform knows just what to do.

There is a little mouse, who resides in the hospital as her house,
And in her house she takes care of all the
sick mice this little nurse mouse.

2013

 MARY MARTINA DOCKTER

THE LITTLEST ANGEL MOUSE

There are many angels in heaven above,
But there is one special angel God does love.

This tiny angel has whiskers and a tail,
And as she flaps her wings her tail does sail.

High above the clouds she flies with ease,
High above the clouds it's like on a trapeze.

When, she watches over the animals, here on earth,
She is their guardian angel on earth since their birth.

She keeps them safe and warm when it's cold,
While they jump and run with joy it is told.

And with the help of Mother Nature nearby,
There'll be plenty of food for those who try.

So, from the tiniest animal to the tallest one of all,
There is one special angel taking care of them all.

This tiny angel has whiskers and a tail,
And as she flaps her wings her tail does sail.

High above the clouds she flies with ease,
High above the clouds it's like on a trapeze.

There are many angels in heaven above,
But, there is one special angel God does love.

For, this tiny angel lives in God's house,
And in heaven her name is the littlest angel mouse.

2013

MARY MARTINA DOCKTER

HUGS AND KISSES MOUSE

There once was a mouse who liked to write just X's and O's,
And that is why wherever he went he played tic-tac-toe.

He would use his sharp teeth to hold a crayon when he would write,
Or he would use his tail when he played in
a box of sand, it was quite a sight.

For, everyone knew of this little mouse and his love of the game,
But some other mice questioned why, and thought it was insane.

Because this little mouse really liked to write just X's and O's,
And that is why wherever he went he played tic-tac-toe.

Soon many a mouse grew tired of this
little mouse and his silly game,
Why, they even stopped playing his game
as they thought it was insane.

Because this little mouse really liked to write just X's and O's,
But no other mouse liked the game the same for they didn't know.

That the little mouse when he played the
game had something to show,
So the little mouse told his special story, and here it goes.

The little mouse stood straight and tall and gave a smile,
And with a loud squeak he told the mice around his own style.

"I really like to write just X's and O's as it goes with many wishes,
For, that is why I play tic-tac-toe, to give out hugs and kisses."

Then many a mouse wanted to play the game just the same,
When the other mice knew the reason why they thought it was sane.

For, there once was a mouse who liked to write just X's and O's,
And whenever he played tic-tac-toe, his hugs and kisses would show.

2013

MARY MARTINA DOCKTER

POLKA DOT PIRATE MOUSE

A legend is told on the open seas,
A legend of old about a mouse you please.

For this mouse is a pirate with his own special ship,
Why, this mouse has a long tail from his adventurous trips.

And on his ship when ever he goes out,
This ship has a sail that all talk about.

Because the ship's sail is so magical one can see for miles,
When the ship's a sail its endeavor is the smiles.

And the story is told of this mouse, who is a pirate,
As the legend of old, that he is nice and not a tyrant.

Oh, he may dress like a pirate when he looks up at the stars,
And he may sound like a pirate when he goes RRRRRRRR.

But this mouse who is a pirate with his own special ship,
Goes, looking for treasure on his adventurous trips.

When out on the open seas he travels for miles,
And the treasure he seeks is for children's smiles.

So that is why this ship has a very special sail,
And why his adventures are a magical tale.

For this mouse who is a pirate loves children a lot,
So this mouse, who is not a tyrant, his ship's sail is of polka dots.

And these polka dots are made of hugs and kisses he shares,
For, this mouse who is a pirate shows he really cares.

There is a legend of old on the open seas,
As a legend told about a mouse you please.

2012

MARY MARTINA DOCKTER

THE HALLOWEEN MOUSE

On Halloween, a magical time of year,
A little mouse,
Who, lives in a haunted house,
Had nothing to wear.

To the costume party,
Where his best friend ghost,
Had won the most,
First prizes he had ever, seen.

"What can I be?"
He thought, and he wiggled his nose,
His whiskers touching his toes,
And he planned, secretly.

"This year I will win,
And ghost will be surprised,
When I win first prize,"
So the little mouse did begin.

He hurried and scurried in front of a mirror,
And gazed, "Should I be a butterfly,
And like a ghost, I can fly."
He imagined winning first prize much clearer.

Then suddenly a spider came from the wall,
And the little mouse couldn't believe his eyes,
He was shocked to see the spider's disguise,
For the spider was a butterfly, wings and all.

So the little mouse started all over again,
Thinking this time I can be a beautiful bird,
And I won't say a word,
Because I know I can win.

When out of the blue, flew in a bat,
But it was a bat wearing a costume of a bird,
And singing as lovely as any bird he has heard,
This little mouse would have never dreamt that.

"Now what do I do?"
Cried the little mouse,
Who, lives in the haunted house,
"Oh, who can I be, Oh, please tell me who."

A brilliant idea came to his head,
I'll be a bee, a buzzing, bumblebee,
I'll win first prize, just wait and see,
Not a butterfly or a bird, I'll be a bee instead.

But outside the window, sitting on a perch,
An owl was dressed as a buzzing, honeybee,
The little mouse blinked and blinked to see,
As he wiped away tears, he decided to no longer search.

The Halloween party was tonight,
And the little mouse had nothing to wear,
So he decided he would go as himself there,
Knowing everyone would laugh at the sight.

MARY MARTINA DOCKTER

As he entered the party much to his surprise,
His best friend ghost was dressed as a ghost when,
He was being himself, himself to win,
And together they won first prize.

Then everyone in the haunted house,
Instead of laughing, clapped with good cheer,
From this day forward and since every year,
He wins the prize, just be yourself, the Halloween mouse.

2011

THE HAUNTED HOUSE MOUSE

This is a story one tells at night,
About a mouse named Max, who lives in a house,
He lives in a house, Max the mouse,
But he is not alone in the house, the house of fright.

For Max the mouse has a very special friend,
His friend is a ghost and together they play,
They play with each other all night and day,
Because, no one dares to enter this house when.

Max the mouse and his friend the ghost make scary sounds,
His friend the ghost says BOO, and Max the mouse squeaks,
And that is why no one ever enters or peeks,
For, they are up in the attic running around.

But sometimes it gets very lonely with nothing to do,
When there is no one to hear them rattle their chains,
So Max the mouse and his friend the ghost wanted a new game,
Just maybe they would let someone in that was new.

Max the mouse and his friend the ghost decided to be quiet,
And then finally a family came in to check out the house,
But they didn't know inside the house was a ghost and a mouse,
When this family with a little boy decided they would try it.

MARY MARTINA DOCKTER

For they didn't mind the noises in the attic with the rattling chains,
Why this new family loved the spooky house,
And they would say to each other we have a ghost and a mouse,
While their little boy played his games.

So Max the mouse and his friend the ghost made scary sounds,
They made scary sounds in the haunted house,
For the family enjoyed their ghost and Max the mouse,
Because they loved having Max the mouse and the ghost around.

2013

THE LITTLEST WITCH MOUSE

Legend tells deep within an enchanted
forest, dwelling under a niche,
There lives a whimsical, little mouse whose
wish is to become a witch.

For a mouse who is a witch, would really be something to see,
As she would wear a tiny witch's hat and fly
a tiny witch's broom with ease.

So this whimsical, little mouse who dwells under a niche,
She enrolls in a magical school in the
enchanted forest to become a witch.

And much to her surprise there were many other
animals with the same idea you see,
They enrolled in the mystic school to become
a witch as they also wanted to be.

But the whimsical, little mouse had to sit
next to the squirming, little squirrel,
Who bothered the whimsical, little mouse
with her tail that constantly twirled!

And the whimsical, little mouse also had to
sit next to the turtle in his shell,
For the turtle bothered the whimsical, little
mouse with his shell where he dwells!

MARY MARTINA DOCKTER

So the whimsical, little mouse decided when
they learn to do their magic spells,
She would cast a spell on the squirrel's tail
to fall off and she would never tell.

And the whimsical, little mouse thought of
a magic spell for the turtle, too,
For she would cast a spell on the turtle's shell
and the turtle would have no clue.

This made the whimsical, little mouse who wanted
to become a witch not a nice mouse,
When at the magic school they only talked about
being a good witch in this school house.

What, was this whimsical, little mouse who
wanted to become a witch to do,
If she wanted to become a witch in the enchanted
forest, she needed to be good, too.

So when the day came and they learned
how to do their magic spells,
This whimsical, little mouse did a nice spell
instead and the squirrel's tail stayed well.

And the whimsical, little mouse did a nice spell
on the turtle's shell where he dwells, too,
For, the turtle stopped bopping his head in and
out of his shell and he didn't have a clue.

When all the animals at the mystical school
graduated and received their brooms,
This whimsical, little mouse wearing her
witch's hat flew across the moon.

Why a mouse who is a witch would really be something to see,
As she wears her tiny witch's hat and flies her tiny broom with ease.

For legend tells deep within the enchanted
forest, dwelling under a niche,
There lives a whimsical, little mouse who
is the nicest, littlest mouse witch.

2012

MARY MARTINA DOCKTER

ELECTION DAY MOUSE

A very clever mouse resides in a very special place,
This very special place is for all religion, gender and race.

Because every four years our nation decides with a vote,
On who will be the next President by a ballet so just take note.

That this very clever mouse who resides in this very special place,
Is very happy every vote counts for all religion, gender and race.

So on Election Day this tiny mouse, who's very, very, clever,
Wiggles his nose and jiggles his toes when
all is in order with the endeavor.

As men and women stand in line to cast their vote for the election,
This very clever mouse never in doubt knows
the history with the selection.

The national day started in the year 1844 for an Election Day,
And it was decided by Congress to be the first
week of November on a Tuesday.

Then farmers were able to finish their harvest
with winter storms reduced,
And many residents were able to travel
without the fear of being a recluse.

This very clever mouse with his tail dancing scampers into his hole,
When, the last person standing cast their vote into the ballet poll.

Because every four years our nation decides with a vote,
On who will be the next President by a ballet so just take note.

That a very clever mouse resides in a very special place,
And this very special place is for all religion, gender and race.

2012

                                        MARY MARTINA DOCKTER

VETERAN'S DAY MOUSE

It's been a tradition in this very unique mouse house,
A special day is celebrated to honor each and every mouse.

Who heard the call and stood tall because they were very brave,
As they sacrificed for their country so they may protect and save.

Our precious freedom we cherish today in each and every home,
And that is why a special day is celebrated
to honor every veteran known.

For within this very unique mouse house,
There lives a mouse with the name of Nicky mouse.

And Nicky mouse was given the name,
As his great grandfather Sgt. Nicholas mouse was the same.

But Nicky mouse who, lives in this very unique
mouse house was uncertain why,
His family celebrates a day to honor the brave
who answered their country's cry.

"Why do we have a special day to honor every veteran known?
I know I was named after my great grandfather
mouse because I am older and have grown."

So father mouse who heard his cry took Nicky mouse aside,
And he began to tell him the story about the
day to honor those who strived.

"We celebrate Veteran's Day to the cause of world peace,
For, it became a legal holiday on November 11,
1918 at the end of World War I siege."

"In the past this day was observed and known as
Armistice Day to honor those in WWI,
But in 1954 Congress amended the act so we
may celebrate and honor everyone."

"Who heard the call and stood tall because they were very brave,
As they sacrificed for their country so they may protect and save."

"Our precious freedom we cherish today in each and every home,
And that is why a special day is celebrated
to honor every veteran known."

Then Nicky mouse who, lives in this very unique
mouse house was especially honored today,
Because he was named after his great grandfather
Sgt. Nicholas mouse who was very, very brave.

And since the end of World War I at this very unique mouse house,
A special day is celebrated to honor each and every mouse.

Who heard the call and stood tall because they were very brave,
And Nicky mouse is now proud to share a special bond
with his great grandfather mouse on this Veteran's Day.

2012

MARY MARTINA DOCKTER

HAPPY THANKSGIVING MOUSE

"There is so much to be thankful for," toasted father mouse,
Today family and friends were gathered together in their house.

And sitting next to her father at the head of the table,
Was his curious daughter little mouse Mabel.

For little Mabel mouse patiently watched her father try,
And carve the biggest turkey she has ever seen with her eye.

So that is why when the turkey was carved all did clap,
As family and friends enjoyed the feast and that was that.

But little mouse Mabel being so curious wanted to know why,
Why do we celebrate Thanksgiving so she gave a sigh?

And decided to ask her father on the couch, who didn't budge,
What the fuss was all about so she gave him a nudge.

It took a couple of pokes before he even started to stir,
To get his attention and ask the question, "What did occur?"

"Dad, we just celebrated Thanksgiving so tell me the story,
I want to hear everything about the holiday even the gory."

"What an imagination you have," chuckled father mouse,
And he cradled his daughter on his lap while in their house.

"The history of Thanksgiving is rooted in English tradition,
It came to this country because of the Pilgrims' omission."

Then little Mabel mouse began to sit a
little taller listening to the tale,
About the Mayflower Ship departing from
England to begin their sail.

"They landed on Plymouth Rock in 1620 to begin a new life,
For, in a new country there is hope of goodness but also strife."

"And because of the Wampanoag Native Americans help in deed,
The Colonists by 1621 learned how to
fish and plant the gift of seed."

"That is why we celebrate Thanksgiving as a feast of harvest good,
We are thankful like the Pilgrims and Indians
were thankful together they stood."

Little mouse Mabel jumped off of her
daddy's lap and started to shout,
"Now I know why we celebrate Thanksgiving
and what the fuss is all about."

"Thanksgiving is the day we celebrate family
and friends with turkey and more,
We gather together to share in the feast we are thankful for."

So every Thanksgiving a toast is made by father mouse,
And little Mabel mouse is the loudest to shout,
"Happy Thanksgiving," in their house.

2012

MARY MARTINA DOCKTER

HAPPY HANUKKAH MICE

In a very special mouse house lives Judah and Judith Mice,
They were always together and best of friends which was very nice.

And the two little mice were doubly excited being they were twins,
For soon in December, Hanukkah, The
Festival of Lights was to begin.

So Judah and Judith Mice scampered
through their house not a bit shy,
They wanted to hear the story again and ask the question why.

"Father, please tell us the history about Hanukkah's holiday start,
We want to know the mystery and please don't leave out any part."

Then father mouse picked up the twins
and placed them on his knee,
"I'll tell you the story my children for there
is no other place I'd rather be."

Judah and Judith Mice were as quiet as a
mouse listening to their dad,
As their father began, "Your names are
very special and I am very glad. "

"The holiday started when Judah the
Maccabee reclaimed the village sight,
As the sacred Temple was cleansed there was
only enough oil for one day's rite."

"Yet according to tradition the oil miraculously
lasted eight days until more was found,
In remembrance the menorah is lit each of the
eight days so Hanukkah was bound."

"And with the help of the beautiful, widowed
Judith, who was also very brave,
We celebrate with cheese and dairy dishes
in honor of her to this day."

"So symbolic of the event we eat traditional
foods fried in oil we make,
Such as latkes, pancakes and now the tradition
of butter cookies and pretzels we bake."

"And don't forget the gifts of coins and the game
of dreidel, a spinning top we play,"
For the twins got very excited about the eight
days of gifts exchanged each day.

When father mouse gave his children a
kiss they began to clap and sing,
Soon there'll be a special prayer, songs, eating
foods, gifts and lighting candles to begin.

For in a very special mouse house lives Judah and Judith Mice,
And together they're known as Happy
Hanukkah mice, which is very nice.

2012

                                        MARY MARTINA DOCKTER

THE BLESSED MANGER MOUSE

In Judea in the town of Bethlehem their lived a tiny mouse,
This tiny mouse made his home in a stable for his house.

And although this stable was somber it did protect from storms,
For all the animals in this stable, it kept them all warm.

So this tiny mouse lived with a cow, a mule and some sheep,
As this is where the innkeeper had his domestic animals to keep.

And together they lived in this stable, sharing straws of hay,
While the cow, the mule and some sheep
ate, this tiny mouse did play.

The story goes in Judea, in the town of Bethlehem,
A man named Joseph and his pregnant wife
Mary had no where to stay, when.

They were travelling from the town of
Nazareth for the census of everyone,
A decree ordered by Caesar Augustus, a count to be done.

And because Joseph was of the lineage of David,
he and his wife Mary were there,
In the town of Bethlehem as that is when this story begins where.

This tiny mouse made his bed with straw in a trough made for feed,
Not knowing this bed of straw would be a manger in need.

While Joseph led his pregnant wife Mary
on a donkey from inn to inn,
The miracle inside the Virgin Mary was soon to begin.

For there was no room for them every innkeeper would say,
But alas an innkeeper told of a stable where they could stay.

And that is when this tiny mouse gave up his bed of straw,
For the Virgin Mary gave birth to her first-born son, a gift for us all.

She wrapped him in swaddling clothes and laid him gently down,
This tiny mouse, a cow, a mule and some
sheep obediently bowed down.

For in Judea, in the town of Bethlehem there
was a stable; an animal house,
That sheltered a cow, a mule and some sheep
and the blessed manger mouse.

2012

　　　　　　　　　　MARY MARTINA DOCKTER

MERRY CHRISTMAS MOUSE

"Christmas is my favorite time of year,"
Merry mouse Marie sang with good cheer.

And she twirled and swirled and danced around,
For, Christmas would soon be coming to town.

When suddenly merry mouse Marie's balance became unsteady,
She stopped her twirling and swirling
because she needed to get ready.

For Christmas would soon be here with its glee,
And there is a lot to do for Christmas, you see.

So merry mouse Marie decided to prepare with a list,
If she had a list, she would not forget or miss.

Everything there is to do to celebrate Christmas,
From the baking, the shopping, and all the decorating fuss.

But as merry mouse Marie thought of all she needed to do,
She became a little leery because she didn't have a clue.

Where to begin with such a long list you see,
And she became very unhappy instead of feeling glee.

"I'll never get done with all there is to do on my list,
This list makes me sad when instead I should feel bliss."

"Christmas is my favorite time of year. I want to feel glad,"
So she tore up the list that made her feel sad.

Because Christmas is more than getting a list done,
Christmas is sharing joy to everyone.

And so she twirled and swirled being she was merry mouse Marie,
For Christmas would soon be coming to town, you see.

2012

                                        MARY MARTINA DOCKTER

A HOLIDAY PLAY BY THE MOUSE BALLET

It is the holiday season in Mouse Town,
And at the mouse dance studio are ballerinas to be found.

For, they are diligently rehearsing for a very special show,
The holiday play of The Nutcracker for everyone in town will go.

The smallest to the largest mouse will all be there to greet,
Why the Mice Theatre where everyone in town will meet.

There on Christmas Eve on that very special night,
The curtains at the Mice Theatre will open
to a ballet of magical delight.

When, the mice orchestra begins to play
"Tchaikovsky's Nutcracker Suite",
The audience of mice grows quiet while some
mice need help to find their seat.

FIRST ACT-
THE PARTY SCENE

It is a glorious, Christmas Eve at the Stahlbaum mouse house,
For, they are hosting their annual Christmas
party for guests of mouse.

A large and beautiful Christmas tree is in the center of the room,
While Clara mouse and Fritz mouse play,
guests will be arriving soon.

Then Mr. and Mrs. Stahlbaum mouse welcome
each and every mouse guest,
As they enter the grand house wearing
their Christmas holiday dress.

The party grows festive as the mice children
play and their parents dance,
When, godfather Drosselmeyer mouse
arrives, bearing gifts that prance.

For Drosselmeyer mouse is a skilled clock maker
and has their curiosity short and tall,
When, he presents two large boxes with magical
toys inside of life size mouse dolls.

They are quite a delight at the party as they swirl and twirl around,
As the mice children begin to open gifts under
the Christmas tree they have found.

Then Drosselmeyer mouse presents Clara
mouse with a beautiful Nutcracker doll,
And Fritz mouse becomes so jealous he
causes it to break by making it fall.

Clara mouse is extremely heart broken and begins to cry real tears,
But Drosselmeyer mouse repairs the Nutcracker
with his handkerchief and ends her fears.

For the evening grows late and the guests of
mice soon depart the mouse house,
And a beloved Nutcracker is safe under the
Christmas tree with the sleeping Clara mouse.

                              MARY MARTINA DOCKTER

THE FIGHT SCENE

She sleeps under the Christmas tree unknowing
to her family that went to bed,
For, she was worried about her beloved
Nutcracker as a dream plays in her head.

The clock strikes midnight when strange
things appear for a mischievous task,
The toys around the Christmas tree turn to life
while the room fills with mean rats.

The rats are led by the fierce Rat King creeping
towards the sleeping mouse child,
As the Nutcracker awakens he leads his army of
toy soldiers to battle the rats gone wild.

The Rat King comers the Nutcracker and fights him one on one,
And the Nutcracker seems to be no match for
the Rat King as the rats have won.

When suddenly Clara mouse makes a final
attempt and throws her slipper in the ring,
Hitting the Rat King on the head, the rats run
away carrying their badly, beaten king.

THE LAND OF SNOW

The Nutcracker becomes a handsome Prince and
takes Clara mouse to the Land Of Snow,
Where, they are welcomed in the enchanted
forest by a dancing snowflake show.

For, on their way to the Land Of Sweets they are
greeted by the Snow Prince and Queen,
And within the enchanted forest is a blanket of
snow where a beautiful ballet is seen.

The Snow Prince, the Snow Queen and
Snowflakes dance as a special treat,
Before, Clara mouse and her Prince travel
beyond to the Land of Sweets.

INTERMISSION: 15 MINUTES
SECOND ACT: LAND OF SWEETS

The Prince escorts Clara mouse to the Land
Of Sweets with surprises to come,
For, they are welcomed in this wonderland by the fairy Sugar Plum.

When, the Prince describes their daring battle
with the rat army and their king,
The Sugar Plum Fairy rewards their effort with
a celebration of dances she'll bring.

Different nationalities will be represented
by several dances of sweets,
Clara mouse and the Prince are happy to
watch so they begin to take their seats.

The dancers' costumes resemble the sweets
they bring from their far off land,
First will be the Spanish mice dance, dressed
in chocolate as they began.

Then in comes two little mice with the Chinese dance we see,
Up, down, up, down on their toes with their
fans waving, they're oriental tea.

The Arabian mice dancers mysteriously begin
while their faces are hidden by a veil,
For, they sway to the music like dancing serpents
and coffee is their countries tale.

The Russian mice dance is quite a step as
the dancers dance on bended knee,
The music is quick as the dancers kick their
legs up like candy canes we see.

A magical dance takes place as Mirliton mice dancers take the stage,
As Clara mouse and the Prince are under the
reed flutes spell, her dream turns a page.

Mother Ginger mouse wears a bon-bon skirt
wrapped around a wonderful surprise,
As she waves to the audience she lifts up her skirt
for her mice children are there inside.

The Waltz of the Flowers is a joyful dance
with mice ballerinas so merry,
And there is also a lovely dance with the
mouse ballerina Dew Drop Fairy.

Then for the grand finale the Sugar Plum Fairy
and the Cavalier, a Pas de Deux dance,
For the magical dream ends as Clara mouse
suddenly wakes up from her trance.

She finds herself under the Christmas tree with
the beloved Nutcracker in her arms,
When she slowly departs the stage the Nutcracker
stands alone with all its charm.

THE END THE CURTAINS CLOSE

The curtains at the Mice Theatre close the ballet of magical delight,
For an audience of mice stand and cheer on this very special night.

The mice performers appear on stage each
taking a bow for their curtain call,
As they proudly smile and wave at the
audience for they have given their all.

At the center of the stage the Sugar Plum
Fairy is presented a rose bouquet,
And then every ballerina is given a red rose
in gratitude, they wish to say.

For it is a glorious, Christmas Eve in Mouse Town,
And the holiday play "The Nutcracker" by the
mouse ballet is the best show around.

2013

THE CHRISTMAS MOUSE

Once there lived a little mouse.
That loved to celebrate the joy of Christmas.
This little mouse lived in a special house.
For the North Pole was his address.

Now, it was told, Jack Frost and Snowflake were his best friends.
The little mouse would snuggle by the fire's blaze.
And watch Jack Frost and Snowflake dance in the wind.
The little mouse enjoyed looking out the window as they played.

Suddenly his little nose would begin to twitch and wiggle.
A delightful aroma was coming from the nearby kitchen.
So he said goodbye to Jack Frost and Snowflake's winter jiggle.
And scampered straight towards what he could snitch, then.

There was Mrs. Claus at her oven to bake.
Delicious cookies were placed on the workers' shelf.
The little mouse scurried, worried he was too late.
He enjoyed sharing the Christmas cookies with the elves.

And so did Santa Claus as he would appear.
The elves and the little mouse would begin to clap.
Ho, Ho, Ho Santa Claus called with good cheer.
As the little mouse enjoyed sitting on Santa's lap.

Christmas was the little mouse's favorite time of year.
All the elves and Mrs. Claus and Santa were in the house.
He would lay by the fireplace with his friends near.
For, he loved that he was the North Pole's Christmas mouse.

2011

SANTA'S LITTLE HELPER MOUSE

Once there was a little mouse who, lived where it was very, very cold,
This little mouse lived at the North Pole the story is told.

And there at the North Pole is where he made his house,
Where, there was always a blanket of white for this little mouse.

For this little mouse loved to play in the snow at the North Pole,
But if it got too cold, he just scampered into his hole.

And that is where this story will begin,
At the North Pole with a little mouse, when.

This little mouse did so much more than just play,
He had an important job to do during the day.

Because Santa Claus was getting ready for his mission to leave,
For that one special night of the year called Christmas Eve.

So this little mouse was very, very busy this time of year,
Not only did he help Santa Claus with his
gear, but he helped feed the deer.

Oh, this little mouse merrily went to each
reindeer stall checking the magic hay,
For it was the magic hay that enabled the reindeer to fly, fly away.

With Santa Claus in his sleigh holding the
reins and a mouse by his side,
Why this little mouse even helped Santa Claus,
check his list twice during the ride.

    MARY MARTINA DOCKTER

And that is where this story will end,
At the North Pole with a little mouse, when.

Once there was a little mouse who lived at the North Pole,
And this little mouse was Santa's little helper the story is told.

2012

HAPPY NEW YEAR MOUSE

Soon after Christmas the decorations
come down in the mouse house,
The holiday is over and a new year will begin for this little mouse.

But this little mouse doesn't believe there is joy in a new year,
When it just seems to him every year ends with a tear.

"For each year starts out the same with resolutions to do,
Why should I celebrate a brand new year
when these won't get done, too?"

So this little mouse decided he won't even
stay up to greet the new year,
He'll just stay at home and be alone without any cheer.

As New Year's Eve got closer many of his
friends wanted to know why,
His invite to the New Year's Eve celebration had no reply.

"I decided this year there'll be a new tradition in this mouse house,
There will be no celebration, no resolutions for this little mouse."

And as New Year's Eve got even closer
this little mouse didn't even try,
To say hello or give a friend a hug, all he could do was sigh.

That is when he realized not to celebrate a
New Year was making him sad,
There really is a lot to be thankful for and
just the thought made him feel glad.

MARY MARTINA DOCKTER

"I'm thankful for my family and friends," and then it came to him,
"My resolution should be to spend more time with them."

Because making a list of things to do just for yourself,
Are reasons why many resolutions, end up with dust on the shelf.

So this little mouse decided he would bring
in the New Year with good cheer,
For this little mouse knew the secret to keep joy all through the year.

Soon after Christmas the decorations
come down in the mouse house,
And joy continues through out the year
with this Happy New Year mouse.

2012

THE JOYOUS KWANZAA MOUSE

Living in the city with her family in their house,
A very special sibling and her name is Moesha mouse.

Moesha mouse has many brothers and sisters you see,
With aunts, uncles and cousins, you might
even say a very large family tree.

So every year the day after Christmas the family plans to come,
And celebrate the seven days of Kwanzaa,
a joyous holiday for everyone.

Now Moesha mouse was especially excited
to see her great nana mouse,
For, she will be coming to help celebrate Kwanzaa in their house.

And as the house was decorated with objects
of art and colorful African cloth,
Her mother, sisters and Moesha mouse will wear
kaftans great nana mouse had brought.

But Moesha mouse being the youngest had never heard the story,
That great nana mouse has told about
the holiday of Kwanzaa's glory.

So Moesha mouse sat next to great nana mouse as did her family,
With her brothers, sisters, aunts, uncles, and
cousins, together to hear you see.

Great nana mouse held Moesha mouse's hand as she began to say,
And greet all with "Habari Gani, what's the news," a Swahili phrase.

     MARY MARTINA DOCKTER

As Moesha mouse sat as quiet as a mouse the
seven principles of Kwanzaa was told,
For the seven days of unity, self determination,
work and responsibility, smart economics,
purpose, creativity and faith to behold.

And as the traditional candle holder, kinaras, was lit,
It represents the symbolic African-American roots as they all sit.

Then during the ceremony Moesha mouse's brothers begin to drum,
And great nana mouse told African history to everyone.

When the musical selections and artistic performances were done,
Great nana mouse finally announced the
feast, Karamu, for all to come.

And to celebrate themselves during the
holiday with family and guests,
For the name Kwanzaa is a Swahili phrase
meaning, "First Fruits of the Harvest".

Moesha mouse gave great nana mouse a
hug and a kiss for now she knew,
Why they observed the holiday of Kwanzaa, too.

And she was filled with pride for her family
in the city living in their house,
A very special, sibling and her name is
Moesha, the joyous Kwanzaa mouse.

2012

I HAVE A DREAM MOUSE

This is a tale about a certain mouse,
Who, remembers an honorable black man who spoke at his house.

For this unusual mouse who is very, very old,
Had witnessed Martin Luther King's famous speech it is told.

So this unique mouse who lives in a very historic place,
Resides in a hole in a hall where all is
welcomed every religion and race.

And on August 28, 1963 this determined
mouse stood on the steps to see,
A very special black man, give a speech for everyone to believe.

Hope in The American Civil Rights Movement
from one man's dream that day,
When many marched with hands held to the
Lincoln Memorial to listen and pray.

As Martin Luther King Jr. gave his, "I have a dream," speech,
This hopeful mouse among the crowd listened
to this noble black man, preach.

The dream of freedom and equality for everyone in this land,
"Now is the time," Martin Luther King spoke as each held a hand.

"We can never be satisfied, for jobs and freedom must come about,"
"With this faith," "Let freedom ring," and "Free
at last," Martin Luther King did shout.

                    MARY MARTINA DOCKTER

And this meek mouse with all who were
there heard what he had to say,
"I have a dream, that my four little children will one day live in a
nation where they will not be judged by the color of their skin
but by the content of their character. I have a dream today."

For this unique mouse who is very, very old,
Had witnessed Martin Luther King's famous speech it is told.

And this is the tale about a certain mouse,
Who, remembers a very special black man,
with a dream, speak at his house.

2013

WISH UPON A STAR MOUSE

Once upon a time but not too long ago it seems,
There was a special, little mouse with a big dream.

For this special, little mouse was unable to use his legs, where,
He was confined to a wheelchair and there he would stare.

He would stare up at the sky when nighttime came around,
So this special, little mouse wished upon a star he had found.

And by his tiny window this special, little mouse wanted to be,
When by his tiny window this special, little mouse was free.

This special, little mouse was free to wish upon a star,
As it was the brightest star in the night, the brightest star by far.

And one would think this special, little mouse's wish would be,
A wish for himself but it was a wish for you and me.

For this special, little mouse was happy where he was at,
This special, little mouse had big dreams where he sat.

And he hoped everyone would realize just how lucky they truly are,
For that is why this special, little mouse wished upon a star.

Because this special, little mouse was unable to use his legs, where,
He was confined to a wheelchair and there he would stare.

　　　　　MARY MARTINA DOCKTER

He would stare up at the sky when nighttime came around,
So this special, little mouse wished upon a star he had found.

For once upon a time but not too long ago it seems.
There was a special, little mouse with a big, big dream.

2013

HAPPY VALENTINE'S DAY MOUSE

In a one room school house,
There lives a very smart, country mouse.

This very small rodent,
He is the school's special student.

He even has his own tiny desk,
It's a match box where his books can rest.

But this smart mouse has one big problem, though,
This very small mouse cannot make scissors, go.

Try and try he would try with all his might,
But in the end his try is a messy, messy sight.

And with Valentine's Day soon to be here,
How will he ever make Valentine cards for his classmates so dear?

Suddenly, a brilliant idea popped into his head,
"I won't use my sharp teeth or my front
hands I'll use my long tail, instead."

"And on Valentine's Day my friends will totally be surprised,
When they see I made them cards, they won't believe their eyes."

So to make sure it was a surprise, he did his art project at night,
He gathered red and white construction paper
and sparkling glitter to do it right.

And by using his tail he was able to do the job just fine,
For instead of being messy, his work was perfect this time.

MARY MARTINA DOCKTER

Then during the day when the other students were making all theirs,
It looked like the smart mouse was just
studying and he really didn't care.

Because on Valentine's Day when everyone
was handing out their cards to wish,
All his classmates will never expect they
were on his Valentine card list.

That evening he placed the Valentine cards on each student's desk,
It took him almost all night and he barely got any rest.

For the small mouse knew this was worth all his hard work,
Just to see their happy faces from his surprise when they looked.

But the next day mouse had the biggest surprise
in this one room school house,
By his desk the best card read, "Happy Valentine's
Day to Our Favorite Country Mouse."

2012

ST. PATRICK'S DAY MOUSE

"Top of the morning," squeaked Tiny O'Shea mouse,
As he went through town passing each mouse house.

It's St. Patrick's Day so he was in a hurry,
Thinking, "I cannot be late," so he surely did worry.

Today is the big day,
The St. Patrick's Day Parade.

And since he was the mayor, the big cheese,
He was in charge of the whole affair, if you please.

So that is why he was in a hurry to scurry,
And not be late for he surely did worry.

For the mayor of Mouse Town was elected to be,
The one to pick out the biggest four leaf clover, you see.

In the St. Patrick's Day Parade that went through the town,
So the biggest four leaf clover must be found.

And there, Mayor O'Shea mouse did yield,
As the mice gathered in the four leaf clover field.

Everyone from Mouse Town was there to help out,
From the wee little pup to the oldest, no doubt.

Because who ever finds the biggest clover in size,
Will be in the parade next to the mayor as their prize.

So they all began searching like busy bumble bees,
Scurrying through the field hoping to be the one to please.

MARY MARTINA DOCKTER

The mayor of Mouse Town looking pious as he stood,
Waiting to judge four leaf clovers that will make him look good.

But there must be a problem, too much time it did take,
For no mice did come up with the clovers to make.

The mayor of Mouse Town in the parade to look good,
So he pretended not to notice and there he just stood.

Then slowly the mice started coming up to claim their prize,
But something was wrong there were only three leaves to the size.

For they found some of the biggest clovers he had ever seen,
But they were not four leaf clovers, not to be mean.

In the crowd of mice a joyful voice did call,
For a wee little pup held a four leaf clover small.

"I found the one, the perfect one to be,
In the parade with the mayor and me."

So the mayor of Mouse Town held the clover up high,
"Yes, this is the one, the perfect one in size."

For size does not have to be the biggest of all,
The perfect size is the heart of the mouse to the call.

And in the St. Patrick's Day Parade that
passed by each mouse house,
Was the mayor of Mouse Town and the St. Patrick's Day, mouse.

2012

THE EASTER MOUSE

Living next door to the Easter Bunny's house,
Was his neighbor Mr. Stingy Mouse.

For even though he was bigger than most other mice,
His name came about because he was meaner than nice.

And that is why his nickname stingy was called,
When, he didn't care to give to others at all.

Mr. Stingy Mouse wasn't a good neighbor, indeed,
He wouldn't even wave to Easter Bunny when he'd leave.

And that was as far as his friendship would go,
Living next door to the Easter Bunny he didn't care to know.

Now when Easter Bunny's neighbors came
to help celebrate Easter day,
Mr. Stingy Mouse would stay home and just say. "Bah Humbug!"

So his living next door to the Easter Bunny's house,
Was, becoming a problem for Mr. Stingy Mouse.

Because days before the holiday at the Easter Bunny's place,
All the other neighbors came over to put
bunny ears on, without haste.

There were Mr. and Mrs. Squirrel and baby squirrels, three,
With Mary the oldest, middle David and tiny Timothy.

The skunks and the beavers and all the other mice,
Except for Mr. Stingy Mouse, who wasn't, very nice.

  MARY MARTINA DOCKTER

All the animals in the forest came to help out,
But not Easter Bunny's one neighbor, a scrooge no doubt.

For he disliked everything to do with Happy Easter Sunday,
But most of all he disliked the Easter Bunny's basket display.

Baskets filled with chocolates, colored Easter eggs and jelly beans,
Just the thought of those baskets made Mr. Stingy Mouse scream.

"How can, the Easter Bunny with his helpers give out,
Give all those Easter baskets to ungrateful children no doubt."

And that is why Mr. Stingy Mouse every Easter stayed away,
Because of those ungrateful children who
receive Easter baskets anyway.

So he decided this year he would spoil Easter Sunday,
By hiding all the Easter baskets the Easter Bunny gives away.

And in the middle of the night he crept to Easter Bunny's house,
For all the other helpers had left except Mr. Stingy Mouse.

Then one by one he hid the Easter baskets away,
So nothing will be there for those children Easter day.

No Easter egg hunt, no baskets filled with joy,
Nothing will be there for those girls and boys.

Nothing but sadness for the first time in years,
This Easter Sunday there'll be nothing but tears.

So Mr. Stingy Mouse decided to stay close by,
To watch for his neighbors and keep an open eye.

As one by one they entered the Easter Bunny's house,
Then one by one they left and hugged Mr. Stingy Mouse.

For instead of angry faces on his neighbors this year,
Instead of sad faces they came with good cheer.

Because the Easter Bunny still had one Easter basket to give,
And the gift was for Mr. Stingy Mouse
hoping his heart would grow big.

If he knew how it felt to receive a gift from a friend,
Then maybe just maybe his hatred would end.

When all of a sudden Mr. Stingy Mouse just knew,
What, giving was like, because his small heart just grew.

And decided from then on to help the
Easter Bunny and friends give out,
Give all the Easter baskets on Easter
Sunday to the children no doubt.

Because living next door to the Easter Bunny's house,
Was his very best neighbor Mr. Easter Mouse.

2012

                    MARY MARTINA DOCKTER

THE LITTLE HELPER MOUSE

Many years ago before your were here,
There was a little apprentice mouse with a tail so dear.

For the story goes this curious mouse was part of history,
As the tale goes he helped Thomas Edison with the mystery.

And because this very unusual mouse was
one of Thomas Edison's helpers,
This very unique mouse was called an assistant to the inventor.

And by his side they worked on the first bulb that gave light,
A very special invention is why one can see at night.

So when the first bulb was made Thomas
Edison gave it to the mouse,
And step by step the little helper mouse carried
it with his tail upstairs in the house.

Only before the excited mouse could make it all the way,
Oh, he was so nervous the mouse's tail gave away.

And at that very moment he dropped the first bulb that gave light,
With this accident Thomas Edison and his
team had to work a day and a night.

But when they were through Thomas
Edison decided more was at stake,
Then the first light bulb that gave light but a
young inventor's heart that did break.

And as Thomas Edison looked around to see
who again should carry the light,
He gave it back to the mouse for surely this
gesture changed his future sight.

For many years ago before you were here,
There was a little apprentice mouse with a tail so dear.

2012

MARY MARTINA DOCKTER

PEANUT BUTTER MOUSE

There once lived a little mouse with the name of Peanut Butter,
He was given the name because he loved
peanut butter more than any other.

For this little mouse could eat peanut butter
breakfast, lunch and dinner,
Being it was his favorite meal and definitely a winner.

So one day when this little mouse had to wait and wait,
The little mouse squeaked, "Why is there
no peanut butter on my plate?"

He cried and cried, "Peanut butter, peanut
butter I would like some more,
Can we please buy more peanut butter at the peanut butter store?"

The little mouse's mom and dad just
smiled and looked at each other,
Then they asked their little mouse son, "Do you
want to know the mystery of peanut butter?"

But little mouse who was very smart thought
he knew peanut butter's history,
He said, "I know about George Washington
Carver, so why is there a mystery?"

"Yes," the little mouse parent's said, "George
Washington Carver was born a slave.
And he became a great scientist of plants and an
inventor. But he did not discover the beginning
of what we now know as peanut butter."

Then little mouse's ears popped up because he wanted to show,
How excited he was to learn the mystery of
peanut butter he wanted to know.

So his parents told him about the Aztec
Indians in the 15" Century then,
And how they ground up peanuts so that
is when peanut butter began.

"Wow," said little mouse he could not believe
peanut butter had been around for so long,
When he just remembered with his stomach
growling that the peanut butter was all gone.

There once lived a little mouse with the name of Peanut Butter,
And he was given the name because he loved
peanut butter more than any other.

2012

          MARY MARTINA DOCKTER

CINCO DE MAYO MOUSE

"Hola, hello," squeaked little Antonio Raton, mouse,
As papa and mama mouse welcomed guests into their casa, house.

For today was Cinco de Mayo, the fifth of May,
A very special fiesta celebration, celebrated today.

But little Antonio Raton wasn't quite sure why,
His family and friends celebrated this day so he gave a sigh.

"What's all the fuss about," he said out loud,
"Why do we celebrate anyway," but no one heard him in the crowd.

At least that is what little Antonio mouse had thought,
With everyone talking too loud about the tamales they had brought.

But someone did hear little Antonio Raton's desperate plea,
For abuelo, grandpa mouse was near enough to hear him, you see.

So grandpa mouse took little Antonio mouse aside from the others,
"I'm going to tell you the history of this day
so the mystery will be uncovered."

Little Antonio Raton was as quiet as a mouse,
As he sat on his grandpa's knee listening in his casa, house.

"Cinco de Mayo," said abuelo mouse, "the fifth of May,
It is not Mexico's Independence Day."

"It's not," whimpered little Antonio mouse, somewhat surprised,
"No," grandpa mouse whispered "and I'll tell you just why."

Little Antonio's eyes grew bigger anticipating what's in store,
For abuelo mouse began to tell him the story
about the Franco-Mexican War.

"Cinco de Mayo is the battle of Puebla in 1862 on the fifth of May,
It's for freedom and democracy, that is why we celebrate today."

"It was Mexico's unlikely victory over French forces," he cried,
"Cinco de Mayo is a celebration of Mexican heritage and pride."

Little Antonio mouse now understood what the fuss was all about,
"Cinco de Mayo is a very special celebration," he began to shout.

"That is why we celebrate with music, dance and a parade,
We have a fiesta celebrating our culture
with family and friends today."

So little Antonio Raton joyfully joined in
the celebration at his casa, house,
And from that day forward every fifth of May he
was known as the Cinco de Mayo mouse.

2012

                                    MARY MARTINA DOCKTER

MOTHER'S DAY MOUSE

Mother's Day was like a holiday in the mouse house,
Because of a very special daughter their little girl mouse.

Little girl mouse loved her mother very, very much,
And Mother's Day was that one day to show her just how much.

But what sort of Mother's Day present should little girl find,
A Mother's Day present, you know, must be one of a kind.

So little girl mouse decided to search through the woods,
To find that special Mother's Day present, hoping she could.

There, growing out from nowhere was a beautiful, red flower,
"A flower" she thought, "A flower will surely shower."

"My mother with happiness on this Mother's Day,
And how much I truly love her, this flower will say."

As little girl mouse went to pick the red rose,
She suddenly remembered the rose tickles her mother's nose.

And little girl sighed, "Oh, this flower won't do, this one red rose,
I'll find something better." So off little girl mouse goes.

For little girl mouse didn't have long to wait,
Why, just there by the river a rock resembled a paper-weight.

"This is it," she thought and scampered back on the path,
But when little girl headed home her joy didn't last.

"It's not really a paper-weight it's only a small rock,"
And she suddenly remembered all those rocks
in her mother's drawer of socks.

"Oh this rock won't do even if it looks great,"
So off little girl mouse goes not wanting to be late.

Next to the woods was a nearby vegetable farm,
"I'll look here," little girl thought, "It won't do any harm."

So little girl mouse went into the garden
this Mother's Day morning,
Forgetting what her parents had said about the farmer's warning.

"A vegetable," she thought, "a vegetable would be just great,
I'll put a vegetable on my mother's, Mother's Day plate."

And as little girl mouse climbed up the stalk so green,
She suddenly remembered her parents
warning the farmer being so mean.

And although the gift she wanted to bring was of corn,
Instead of finding the right present, she would have been scorned.

So back to the woods little girl mouse went to look,
For it was getting late and too much time she thought it took.

To find that special present for her mother on Mother's Day,
Just one more try, I'll try, for that special present today.

So little girl mouse followed the path back through the woods,
And there it was the perfect present in front of her as she stood.

   MARY MARTINA DOCKTER

"A star," she thought, "a star will be the right one,"
And little girl mouse started for home
because she thought she was done.

But when she picked up the star that was only a leaf,
Because of her sharp teeth the star's life was only brief.

"Now what do I do", as the leaf crumbled without a sound,
With only the stem between her teeth, the
broken leaf fell to the ground.

Today is Mother's Day and little girl mouse had nothing to bring,
But when little girl mouse went home crying she decided to sing.

"I'll sing," she thought, "I'll sing to my mother for Mother's Day,
For a present from the heart is the best gift to give today."

Mother's Day was a very special day in the mouse house,
Because of a Mother's Day gift by their little girl mouse.

2012

MEMORIAL DAY MOUSE

"Why do we collect red poppies?" Questioned Jr., mouse,
As he helped his mother, gather the small
flowers growing near their house.

"Because today is a very special day," sighed his tearful mother,
And seeing his mother crying mouse Jr. began to wonder.

"Why is today so special when you seem so sad."
"Well my son today is the day we honor those
who have fallen just like your dad."

"My dad was a war hero," mouse Jr. said as he stuck out his chest,
"Yes my son, he was very brave just like the rest."

"Today we decorate the graves of those
who have sacrificed their lives,
It is on Memorial Day we honor the men
and women who have died."

"So that is what the red poppies are for,
To remember the brave men and women who have died in war."

Then mouse Jr. started to gather the red poppies even faster,
When a question suddenly popped into
his head he wanted to ask her.

"Who started Memorial Day, anyway?" A
concerned mouse Jr. squeaked,
"Well," mother mouse replied, and then thought, "let me see."

                    MARY MARTINA DOCKTER

"Memorial Day was proclaimed on
May 5, 1868 by General John Logan,
But it wasn't until May 30, 1868 at Arlington
National Cemetery it officially began."

Mouse Jr. sat and listened as his mother told the story,
About the Civil War and flowers placed
on the soldiers' graves for glory.

And mother mouse cried, "That is why we
distribute the red poppies today,
To honor the fallen soldiers and to help
the veterans in need, we pray."

For it was then Jr., mouse started to wear a red
poppy this day picked near his house,
And from that day forward he was proud to be
known as the Memorial Day mouse.

2012

FATHER'S DAY MOUSE

Father's Day was the best day ever in the mouse house,
Because of a very special son, their big boy mouse.

Big boy mouse loved his father very, very much,
And Father's Day was that one day to show him just how much.

But what sort of Father's Day present should big boy find,
A Father's Day present, you know, must be one of a kind.

So big boy mouse decided to search around the house,
To find that special Father's Day present for his father mouse.

There growing out from under the porch was a bunch of weeds,
"Maybe under the porch I'll find the present I will need."

He pulled and pulled until the weeds were gone,
But when he looked under the porch for
a present there wasn't even one.

So big boy mouse decided to search around the house again,
To find that special Father's Day present for father mouse when.

In the front yard he noticed the grass had grown very tall,
"Maybe under the grass I'll find that present after all."

He pushed and pushed the lawn mower until the grass was cut,
And he looked around the front yard still no present, but.

He noticed in the backyard it looked the same way,
"Maybe this time under the grass I'll find a present today."

 MARY MARTINA DOCKTER

So he pushed and pushed the lawn mower again in hopes to find,
That special Father's Day present for father mouse this time.

But when big boy mouse finished the job
there wasn't a present found,
And father mouse came running out of the
house because of the loud sound.

Big boy mouse without even knowing gave
father mouse that special present,
For father mouse couldn't believe his eyes
because the yard looked so very pleasant.

"Thank you big boy mouse for the best
gift you could have given me."
For big boy mouse helping around the house was his present to be.

So Father's Day was the best day ever in the mouse house,
Because of a very special, helpful son, their big boy mouse.

2012

PAUL REVERE'S RIDE AND
THE MOUSE BY HIS SIDE

Many have heard the story of Paul Revere's ride,
But, have you heard the story of a little mouse by his side.

For Paul Revere was a well known silversmith by his trade,
And it's where this little mouse became
his friend and there he stayed.

A little mouse he kept in his pocket and would take everywhere,
Why, this little mouse he named Liberty would also be there.

On that famous ride Paul Revere secretly did make,
To warn the Colonial Militia, that British forces were at stake.

When on April 18, 1775, Paul Revere heard
The British were about to embark,
And Liberty mouse in Paul Revere's pocket also heard the remark.

That, British forces from Boston were bound
for Lexington and Concord,
To capture founding fathers Samuel Adams and
John Hancock as they headed towards.

The two routes the 700 British soldiers could possibly make,
By, land through the Boston Neck or by sea
across the Charles River they could take.

So Paul Revere and Liberty mouse began
making plans to alert the countryside,
With one if by land and two if by sea lanterns lit
in the Old North Church as they ride.

                    MARY MARTINA DOCKTER

Together with William Dawes and Samuel
Prescott they began their nighttime alarm,
They were to rouse the minutemen of an attack
and warn the citizens of eminent harm.

Then Paul Revere and Liberty mouse
rode to Lexington to persuade,
Ole Samuel Adams and John Hancock to leave
the city for safety from where they stayed.

And Paul Revere with Liberty mouse in his pocket
warned many patriots along this route,
When, many set out on horseback themselves to
deliver warnings of their own no doubt.

For many have heard the story of Paul Revere's ride,
But have you heard the story of a little mouse by his side.

A little mouse he kept in his pocket and would take everywhere,
Why this little mouse he named Liberty who would also be there.

On that famous ride Paul Revere secretly did make,
To warn the Colonial Militia, that British forces were at stake.

2013

THE FOURTH OF JULY MOUSE

In our nation's capital lives a very unique mouse,
This very unusual mouse resides in a very special house.

He was born on the 4th of July, our independence day,
In a tiny hole there within the walls where Congress stays.

And ever since he was young he and his dad would go,
There to watch the men and women in a political show.

Now he was older and he wanted to know why,
His father would want him to watch these politicians' cry.

"Dad, what is so important about being in this room,
When all I hear is men and women talking gloom."

His father just smiled and began to whisper in his ear,
"We are watching our nation in action here."

"This is where it all began,
As men debated over a new country's plan."

So a very skeptical mouse wiggled even closer to his dad,
He wanted to hear the story his father had.

"Son, you were born on the 4th of July, a very special day,
It was the legal separation of the thirteen
colonies form Great Britain's way."

"On July 2, 1776, the Second Continental
Congress voted for independence,
But not until July 4, 1776 was it finally approved
as The Declaration of Independence."

					MARY MARTINA DOCKTER

"That is why I take you here to watch
these men and women in debate,
It is how our country started and became so great."

Then his son squeaked, "And we celebrate with
family, friends, fireworks and parades,
For, we are thankful for our freedom on America's birthday."

When in our nation's capital, there is a very special house,
And living within its walls is the 4th of July Mouse.

2012

THE STATUE OF LIBERY MOUSE

There is a mouse, a very exceptional mouse
and she lives in a very special home,
This very special house where this very
exceptional mouse lives is quite known.

For this very exceptional mouse makes her
house by The Statue of Liberty,
And the Statue of Liberty a famous landmark
is where man and mouse come to see.

The robed female figure, Libertas, representing
the Roman goddess of freedom,
It was a gift from the people of France as
a symbol of hope to welcome.

Every mouse, man, woman and child to
this great and prosperous land,
And that is why this very exceptional mouse
wants every one to understand.

This lady sculpture in New York's Harbor for what she represents,
For, she bears a torch and a tablet with the
inscription of the date of our independence.

And a broken chain lies at her feet to break the bonds of slavery,
When, the people of the United States
are bonded together by bravery.

So this very exceptional mouse is proud to
live by such a wonderful sight,
As, a silent sentinel while many come to
visit Liberty Island day and night.

     MARY MARTINA DOCKTER

And there to read the simple poem that welcomes all to this land,
For The Statue of Liberty carries the torch
welcoming every mouse and man.

"Give me, your tired, your poor, your huddled
masses, yearning to breathe free,
The wretched refuse of your teeming shore, send these, the
homeless, tempest lost to me, I lift my lamp beside the golden door."
For there is a mouse, a very exceptional mouse
and she lives in a very special home,
And this very special house where this very
exceptional mouse lives is quite known.

For this very exceptional mouse makes her
house by The Statue of Liberty,
And The Statue of Liberty a famous landmark
is where man and mouse come to see.

And that is why this very exceptional mouse
wants every one to understand,
The Statue of Liberty welcomes every
mouse and man to this great land.

2013

HERITAGE HISTORY MOUSE

Long ago when our country was new,
There was a special place where mice and people went through.

And in this place there lived many a mouse,
That helped to make this special place a welcome house.

For it is known as Ellis Island this place of old,
As it is where generations of mice and men
came to this country it is told.

And that is where this story will begin,
About a very special mouse and a very special girl when.

On January 1, 1892 Ellis Island became a screening station,
So on opening day mice, men, women
and children came with elation.

For, they had traveled many long miles across the sea on a ship,
To follow their dream for freedom, that is
why they made such a difficult trip.

And there to welcome our country's new citizens was many a mouse,
That helped to make a special place for
immigrants in this heritage history house.

But there was one little mouse and one
young girl in this story of old,
And their names were Annie mouse and
Annie Moore the story is told.

                    MARY MARTINA DOCKTER

For on opening day a special gift was given to
the first immigrant to pass through,
When the gates of Ellis Island opened Annie
mouse was first and Annie Moore, too.

Annie mouse was presented ten golden kernels
of com from the commissioner mouse,
And Annie Moore was given a ten dollar gold
piece when she entered this new house.

Oh, Annie mouse wiggled her nose and
jiggled her tail when she had won,
And Annie Moore just fifteen years old said,
"She will never part with it, but will always keep it
as a pleasant memento of the occasion."

For long ago when our country was new,
There was a special place where mice and people went through.

And there to welcome our country's new citizens was many a mouse,
That helped to make a special place for
immigrants in this heritage history house.

2012

THE WHITE HOUSE MOUSE

There is a notable mouse who, lives in a very special home,
And this very special home is the White House known.

Because this unique mouse resides at
1600 Pennsylvania Avenue to be exact,
As that is the address of the White House residence for a fact.

And this stately mansion with all its glory
began from one cherry tree,
For it is called the presidential White House in Washington D.C.

And it is there this tiny creature makes his
home in the "People's House",
Where George Washington, the first President of the
United States selected the site for man and mouse.

So now this renowned mouse can choose
from 132 rooms to run and play,
When there are so many rooms to choose from throughout the day.

He scrunches his nose and wiggles his tail when
through the entrance hall he runs,
He runs and runs through all the different
rooms, which is a lot of fun.

For the White House has, a Red Room, a Blue
Room and a Green Room to choose from,
But this unique mouse has a certain room
that is his very favorite one.

                    MARY MARTINA DOCKTER

Because this tiny, little mouse has one
very, very special room you see,
And that is the Oval Office where the
President of the United States will be.

So when this little ball of fur scurries into
the room as quiet as a mouse,
He doesn't want to disturb the President of the
United States in the White House.

And there he sleeps in peace this mouse his life of mystery,
For, this simple, little mouse sleeps in a very special house of history.

Where, the President of the United States
is elected to serve man and mouse,
And that is why this peaceful creature is happy
to be the White House mouse.

For there is a notable mouse who lives in a very special home,
And this very special home is the White House known.

Because this unique mouse resides at
1600 Pennsylvania Avenue to be exact,
As that is the address of the White House residence for a fact.

2013

LABOR DAY MOUSE

Across America in every mouse house,
There is an American worker and a working mouse.

But this is a story about one special mouse,
Who lives in a factory and the factory is his house.

He lives in a hole in a very large room,
And he comes and goes at his work I assume.

Because people are too busy to see that he is there,
He is able to come and go at his work without a care.

Then one day he was visited by a mouse from the street,
Who, just came by hoping there was something to eat.

So he opened his front door to let the mouse in,
Why, he wanted to be nice to all mice as a friend.

And share in his good fortune of the American dream,
Because he knew there were some mice not as fortunate it seemed.

When together they nibbled on a big piece of cheese,
His new found friend asked the question, "please."

"Please tell me how you came to this very large place,
You're just one tiny mouse in a house that is safe."

"I don't see any people walking around,
You can come and go and not worry you'll
be stomped to the ground."

                    MARY MARTINA DOCKTER

The very special mouse just chuckled and smiled,
"This very large place is a factory full of people all the while."

"But today is an important day for all who work in this place,
Today is Labor Day and that is why this place is so safe."

"Because the American worker once worked
12 hour shifts seven days a week,
And even children toiled the mines and
factories making them very weak."

"So the Labor Movement in the 1800's created
this holiday for those who work the call,
And on the 1st Monday in September, Labor
Day pays tribute to them all."

His mouse friend then scratched his furry
head with whiskers by his nose,
"So that is why the end of summer is celebrated
with barbeque parties," he goes.

For across America in every mouse house,
There is an American worker celebrating
Labor Day with a working mouse.

2012

THE AMERICAN FLAG MOUSE

There is a patriotic mouse that makes his home by a flag pole,
And this patriotic mouse by the flag pole lives in a hole.

He lives in a hole by the flag pole so he may see,
When, every morning, the American Flag is raised for you and me.

He stands at attention with his hand over
his heart as the flag flies high,
Because, he is proud of his country and
that is why a tear is in his eye.

For the American Flag represents so much
more and it should be taught,
Did you know, the thirteen horizontal stripes, the seven red
alternating with six white are for the original colonies that fought?

And the stars white on a blue field represented a,
"New Constellation", When, the shape, design and
arrangement of the flag allowed for a new state admission.

But the patriotic mouse discovered what
the American Flag also stands for,
For he learned the red in our flag symbolizes hardiness and valor.

While the white symbolizes purity and innocence,
The blue in our flag represents justice, perseverance and vigilance.

And that is why he is proud of his country with a tear in his eye,
As he stands at attention with his hand over
his heart as the flag flies high.

                    MARY MARTINA DOCKTER

Because this patriotic mouse lives in a hole
by the flag pole so he may see,
When, every morning, the American Flag is raised for you and me.

And this patriotic mouse lives in his house by a flag pole to this day,
For this patriotic mouse is proud of his
country and the American Flag.

2013

THRICE AS NICE

Thrice is just as nice when, children entice.
Their imagination soars childhood explores.
For dreams set sail as they cherish fairytales.

Thrice is just as twice when bees give advice.
As, sister and brother buzz by, when they fly.
And having fun can be learning what you see.

Thrice is just as mice when a mouse is as nice.
As you and me can be as we read their stories.
It's a book of poetry, chapters one, two, three.

2021

MARY MARTINA DOCKTER